Midwives On-Call at Christmas

*Mothers, midwives and mistletoe—
lives changing for ever at Christmas!*

Welcome to Cambridge Royal Hospital—
and to the exceptional midwives
who make up its special Maternity Unit!

They deliver tiny bundles of joy on a daily
basis, but Christmas really is a time for
miracles—as midwives Bonnie, Hope,
Jessica and Isabel are about to find out.

Amidst the drama and emotion of babies
arriving at all hours of the day and night,
these midwives still find time for some
sizzling romance under the mistletoe!

This holiday season, don't miss the festive,
heartwarming spin-off to the dazzling
Midwives On-Call continuity
from Mills & Boon Medical Romance:

A Touch of Christmas Magic
by Scarlet Wilson

Her Christmas Baby Bump
by Robin Gianna

Playboy Doc's Mistletoe Kiss
by Tina Beckett

Her Doctor's Christmas Proposal
by Louisa George

Dear Reader,

I was really delighted to be asked to take part in the Midwives On-Call at Christmas series—as you might have guessed by now, I like nothing better than writing Christmas books!

It seemed fitting that my heroine was from Scotland, and I loved the thought of her putting her past behind her and trying to build a new and exciting future for her and her daughter.

Jacob was a whole different matter… The first thing I did was visualise his house and how empty it looked without any love or significant others in it. It was so easy to imagine how gorgeous it might look for Christmas, and a whole part of the story is built around this idea.

Wishing you all a wonderful time—whatever your celebrations at this time of year. I will be frantically wrapping presents, trying to buy Christmas food and hoping I haven't forgotten anything!

Please feel free to contact me at my website: scarlet-wilson.com.

Best wishes,

Scarlet

A TOUCH OF CHRISTMAS MAGIC

BY
SCARLET WILSON

First published in Great Britain 2015
by Mills & Boon, an imprint of Harlequin (UK) Limited,
Eton House, 18-24 Paradise Road, Richmond, Surrey, TW9 1SR

© 2015 Harlequin Books S.A.

ISBN: 978-0-263-25920-9

Special thanks and acknowledgement are given to Scarlet Wilson
for her contribution to the Midwives On-Call at Christmas series

Harlequin (UK) Limited's policy is to use papers that are natural,
renewable and recyclable products and made from wood grown in
sustainable forests. The logging and manufacturing processes conform
to the legal environmental regulations of the country of origin.

Printed and bound in Great Britain
by CPI Antony Rowe, Chippenham, Wiltshire

Scarlet Wilson wrote her first story aged eight and has never stopped. Her family have fond memories of *Shirley and the Magic Purse*, with its army of mice all with names beginning with the letter 'M'. An avid reader, Scarlet started with every Enid Blyton book, moved on to the Chalet School series and many years later found Mills & Boon. She trained and worked as a nurse and health visitor, and currently works in public health. For her, finding Mills & Boon Medical Romances was a match made in heaven. She is delighted to find herself among the authors she has read for many years. Scarlet lives on the West Coast of Scotland with her fiancé and their two sons.

Books by Scarlet Wilson

Mills & Boon Medical Romance

Rebels with a Cause
The Maverick Doctor and Miss Prim
About That Night...

The Boy Who Made Them Love Again
West Wing to Maternity Wing
A Bond Between Strangers
Her Christmas Eve Diamond
An Inescapable Temptation
Her Firefighter Under the Mistletoe
200 Harley Street: Girl from the Red Carpet
A Mother's Secret
Tempted by Her Boss
Christmas with the Maverick Millionaire
The Doctor She Left Behind

Visit the Author Profile page at millsandboon.co.uk for more titles.

This book is dedicated to my fabulous fellow authors
Louisa George, Tina Beckett and Robin Gianna.

It's been a pleasure working with you, ladies!

Praise for
Scarlet Wilson

'*Her Christmas Eve Diamond* is a fun and interesting
read. If you like a sweet romance with just a touch of
the holiday season you'll like this one.'

—HarlequinJunkie

'*West Wing to Maternity Wing!* is a tender, poignant
and highly affecting romance that is sure to bring a
tear to your eye. With her gift for creating wonderful
characters, her ability to handle delicately and
compassionately sensitive issues and her talent
for writing believable, emotional and spellbinding
romance, the talented Scarlet Wilson continues to
prove to be a force to be reckoned with in the world of
contemporary romantic fiction!'

—CataRomance

CHAPTER ONE

THE LITTLE FACE stared back out of the window as Freya gave her a nervous wave from the new school. Bonnie sucked in a breath and kept the smile plastered to her face, waving back as merrily as she could. *Please be okay.*

Her thick winter coat was stifling her already. Even at this time of year, Cambridge was unexpectedly warmer than Scotland. She could feel an uncomfortable trickle of sweat run down her spine. The teacher came to the window and, glancing at Bonnie, ushered Freya away. Freya's red curls had already started to escape from the carefully styled pleat. By the time she came home later her hair would be back to its usual fluffy head style. She could almost hear the teacher's thoughts in her head: *over-anxious parent.*

She wasn't. Not really. But travelling down from Scotland yesterday with their worldly goods stuffed into four suitcases was hardly ideal. The motel they'd ended up staying in was even less pleasant. The smell of damp and mildew in the room had set off alarm bells that it might cause a flare-up of Freya's asthma. With Christmas not too far away, she desperately needed to sort out somewhere more suitable to stay. And the combination of everything, plus dropping Freya at a brand-new school this morning, had left her feeling rattled.

The director of midwifery at Cambridge Royal Maternity Unit had been quite insistent on her start date. No compromise. The ward sister had just taken early maternity leave due to some unexpected problems. They needed an experienced member of staff as soon as possible. And she hadn't felt in a position to argue—despite the fact they'd had nowhere to stay. The job in Cambridge was her way out of Scotland. And, boy, did she need out.

Working at such a prestigious hospital was appealing. Everyone knew about the two-hundred-year-old hospital and one night, midway between tears and frustration, she'd applied. When they'd emailed back the next day to arrange a telephone interview she'd been surprised. And when they'd told her the next day she had the job she'd been stunned. Things had moved at a rapid pace ever since. References, occupational health forms and a formal offer telling her they wanted her to start straight away.

Thankfully, she'd had a sympathetic community manager in Scotland who knew about her circumstances and had done a little jigging to allow her to take annual leave and special leave to let her only work two weeks' notice. The last two weeks had passed in a complete blur.

This morning had been hard. There had been tears and sniffles from Freya, a normally placid child. Bonnie held her breath. The school window remained empty; it was clear the teacher had successfully distracted her.

With a sigh of relief she glanced at her watch. Yikes. First day and she was going to be late. She hurried back to the bus stop. Getting a car was next on the 'to do' list. She phoned and left a message on the director of midwifery's answerphone—hardly a good start for her first day on the job. But it couldn't be helped. The woman knew she wasn't arriving until last night and that her daughter was starting a new school today. She still had to hand some paperwork into HR and pick up her uniforms before she could start on the labour ward.

For once, she was in luck. The bus appeared almost immediately. Now it was daylight and she could actually see a bit of the beautiful city she'd decided to live in on almost a whim.

Well, a whim that was a result of catching her husband in bed with her best friend. She should still feel angry and hurt. But all she really felt was relief. As soon as the ink was dry on the divorce papers she'd started job hunting. She needed a fresh start and there was something so exciting about coming to a historic city like Cambridge. She watched as the Victorian-style shops and Grade II listed buildings whizzed past and allowed herself to smile a little. Cambridge was truly an atmospheric city; seeing it in daylight made her all the more excited to get a chance to see round about.

The hospital came into a view. A large, imposing building based in the heart of the bustling city. A little tremor of anticipation went down her spine. This was it. This was where she worked. As the bus drew to a halt, climbing down, she took a final glance around the city of Cambridge. *Her city.* Full of possibilities.

This was now home.

Jacob Layton was more than mildly irritated. He was mad—but, these days, that was nothing unusual for him.

He hated disorganisation. Hated chaos. He prided himself on the fact that his unit ran like clockwork. Any midwife or medic not up to the job at this hospital was quickly rooted out and dealt with.

It might sound harsh. But in Cambridge Royal Maternity Unit the lives of women and babies were on the line every day. He was a firm believer that all expectant mothers deserved the best possible care and it was his job to ensure they got it.

This morning, he stood at the nurses' station with his hands on his hips as his temper bubbled just beneath the surface. There was no sign of any member of staff. None of the whiteboards were up to date—he didn't even know which patient was in which room. Case notes were spread all over the desk with a whole variety of scribbled multicoloured sticky notes littering the normally immaculate desk.

'Where is everyone?' he yelled.

The frightened faces of a midwife and junior doctor appeared simultaneously from separate rooms. The midwife hurried towards him, her eyes fixed on her shoes. The junior doctor walked slowly, obviously hoping the midwife would get the brunt of Jacob's rage this morning. He should be so lucky.

The midwife handed over a set of notes with slightly shaking hands. 'I think this is the set of notes you wanted. I was just doing Mrs Clark's observations. Everything seems fine.'

He snatched them from her hands and reviewed them quickly. Relief. Things were looking better for Mrs Clark. He raised his head, keeping his voice in check. 'Good. Tell Mrs Clark I'll be in to see her shortly.'

The midwife disappeared in a flash. The junior doctor's legs practically did a U-turn in the corridor. He didn't want to be left with Jacob.

'Dr Jenkins.'

The young guy's legs froze midstride. Jacob flung case notes onto the desk one after another. 'Ms Bates needs her bloods done, Mrs Kelly needs her bloods repeated, where is the cardiac consult for Lucy Evans—she's been here more than six hours—and how long ago did I ask you to arrange another ultrasound for Ms Shaw? Get it done, now!' His voice rose as the anger he was trying to contain started to erupt. He hated incompetence. These patients were in the best maternity unit for miles. They should be receiving top-quality care.

The doctor's face paled and he gathered up the notes in his arms. 'Right away, Dr Layton,' he said, practically scampering down the corridor to the nearest office.

He sighed. This place—normally his pride and joy—was becoming a disaster zone.

Ever since he'd diagnosed the ward manager with pre-eclampsia and sent her home with the instructions not to come back until she had her baby, this place had gone to pot. There were four other senior midwives. All of them excellent at clinical care—and none with an organisational bone in their body.

The director of midwifery had promised him that their new employee would be able to help with all this. But he'd just read her CV, and was struggling to see why a Scottish community midwife would be able to do anything to help a busy city labour ward.

But the thing that was really making him mad was the fact that she wasn't here. He glanced at his watch again. First day on a new job—after nine-thirty—and the new start wasn't here.

The doors at the bottom of the corridor swung open right on cue. Bonnie Reid. It had to be. Jacob knew everyone who worked here and he didn't recognise her at all. Dressed in the blue scrubs that the labour ward midwives wore and bright pink trainers, she had her red hair coiled up on top of her head in a strange kind of knot. How on earth did she do that? That, coupled with the curves not hidden by the shapeless scrubs, reminded him of a poster he'd had on his wall as a teenager. He felt a smile form on his lips.

Was she nervous? Her hands fidgeted with her security pass and she seemed to make a conscious effort to slow her steps. What irritated him most of all was the fact she didn't seem to notice him standing, waiting for her. Instead, she stopped at every room on the way along the corridor, nodding and introducing herself to the members of staff. She even disappeared for a second to obviously help with a patient.

Then, she appeared with a load of laundry, which she put into the laundry bags, reorganised two of the hand scrubs outside the doors and tidied the top of the cardiac-arrest trolley on her way past.

He waited until she'd almost reached him. 'Bonnie Reid?' His voice dripped with sarcasm. 'Nice of you to finally join us.'

Something flickered across her face. Her skin was pale under the bright hospital lights and he could see a few tiny freckles under her make-up. She'd looked good from a distance. Up close, she was much more interesting.

She had real knockout eyes. Dark, dark blue. Not the pale blue normally associated with a redhead. But then her hair wasn't the average red either. It was a dark deep auburn. The kind of colour normally associated with Hollywood actresses who probably had a whole team of people to get it that colour. Almost instantly he knew that Bonnie Reid's was entirely natural. She gave him the slightest glance from those eyes. And for the first time, in a long time, he took a deep breath.

It had been a long time since a woman had ignited something in his system. Maybe it was her dark blue eyes against her pale skin? Or the look of disdain she gave him as she walked past into the treatment room and started washing her hands.

Had he just imagined it? No. Something in her eyes told him this was a woman who had lived—had experienced life. She must be in her early thirties. As she finished washing her hands he glanced at her finger—no ring. It had been a long time since he'd done that too.

She turned to face him. 'Bonnie Reid, new midwife at Cambridge Royal Maternity Unit.' Her eyebrows rose. 'And you are?'

It was her tone. It rankled him right away. He'd never been a person to pull rank. 'Jacob Layton, Head Obstetrician, CRMU.'

It was almost as if a box of chocolates or tray of cakes had appeared out of thin air at the nurses' station. Just about every door in the corridor opened and a whole host of previously hidden staff appeared. Did they avoid him every morning?

Bonnie didn't appear to notice. She blinked and pointed towards his scrubs. 'You should wear an ID badge, Dr Layton. You could be absolutely anyone. I expect all staff members I work with to be clearly identified.'

She was just here. His skin prickled. Patience was not his friend. In any other set of circumstances he might have said their new staff member had an attitude problem. But he got the distinct impression that Bonnie Reid was only reacting to his initial barb.

He didn't know whether to give her a dressing-down or to smile. 'It's Jacob,' he said quietly. 'Everyone calls me Jacob.' Not true. Only the few people not terrified by him called him Jacob. For a second their gazes meshed. It startled him, sending a little jolt around his system.

More than a year. That was how long it had been since he'd felt a spark with someone.

She gave the slightest nod of her head and extended her hand towards his. 'Bonnie. Everyone calls me Bonnie.'

As soon as he connected with her skin he knew he'd made a mistake. The warm feeling of her palm against his. Touch. That was what he'd missed most of all in the last year. The warmness of someone's touch. He pulled his hand back sharply as her eyes widened at his reaction.

'You're late.' It came out much snappier than he intended. Her hand was still in mid-air, suspended from their shake. She drew it back slowly and her gaze narrowed as she took a deep breath and her shoulders went back.

She met his gaze full on. 'Yes, I'm late.' It was clear she had no intention of giving anything else away. He couldn't believe how much one meeting with one woman could irk him.

She was new. She was working in his unit. And, after talks with the director of midwifery, this was the person he was supposed to offer a promoted post to. *If* he deemed her suitable. Tardiness was not an option.

He felt his normal persona resume. The one that had held most of the staff at arm's length for the last year. 'Staff and patients rely on us. Lateness is not acceptable at CRMU. I expected you here at nine a.m.'

It was the first time she looked a little worried. 'I had to take my daughter to school. We arrived late last night from Scotland. She was upset. I had to make sure she was okay.' She glanced over her shoulder as if she expected someone else to be there. 'I left a message for the director of midwifery—she knew my circumstances.'

Those words annoyed him. He'd seen her CV, but the

director hadn't told him anything about their new employee's 'circumstances'. He hated it when staff used excuses for not being able to do a shift, or being late for work.

'We all have circumstances. We all still have to be at work for nine. Work is our priority. Patients are our priority.'

Her face flamed and her eyes sparked. 'Patients are always my priority and I've already dealt with two on my way along the ward. Exactly how many have you dealt with while you've been standing there waiting for me to arrive? Hardly a good use of consultant time.'

She was questioning him. She was challenging him and she'd only been here five minutes. He'd love to sack her on the spot. But they desperately needed the staff right now, and if she was as competent as she was mouthy he'd be in serious trouble with the director of midwives. She was almost questioning his competence. Let them see how she was when someone questioned hers.

'I saw from your CV that you were a community midwife in Scotland. It's a bit of a leap coming to work in an inner city labour ward. Don't you think that might stretch your current capabilities? Are you going to have to refresh your skills?'

It was a reasonable question. At least he felt it was. He still wasn't entirely sure why the director thought a community midwife was a suitable replacement for their ward sister.

It took about a millisecond to realise he'd said exactly the wrong thing.

Bonnie glared at him and put her hands on her hips. 'Please do not question my capabilities or qualifications. In the last year, I've dealt with a shoulder dystocia, umbilical cord prolapse, two women who failed to progress, a footling breech, a cervical lip and an intrapartum haemorrhage. Is that enough for you?' She turned to walk away, then obviously decided she wasn't finished. 'And just so we're clear—' she held out her hands '—I didn't have a fancy unit, staffed with lots of other people to help me. These were home deliveries. I was on my own, with no assistance. Still think I need to *refresh my skills*?'

Her pretty brow was marred by a frown and he could practically feel the heat sparking from her eyes. It was an impressive list—even for a midwife based in a busy labour ward. For a community midwife, some of those situations must have been terrifying. He had a whole new respect for his new midwife.

But Bonnie wasn't finished. It was obvious he'd lit a fire within her and probably touched a nerve. Maybe she was nervous about starting work in a new hospital? Worse, he'd just called her qualifications into question in front of the rest of the staff. He hadn't even considered that might not be entirely appropriate—especially when these could be the people she would be in charge of. Mentally, he was kicking himself.

'My experience with women isn't just in the labour suite, *Dr* Layton.' Oh, boy, she was mad. It was clear, if he was patronising her, they weren't on first-name terms. 'I've spent the last ten years looking after women from the moment they're pregnant until long after the baby is delivered. I've picked up on lots of factors that affect their pregnancy, both clinical and social. And as a community midwife I've dealt with lots of post-delivery problems for both mother and child. Looking after patients at home is a whole lot different from looking after them in a clinical setting. Isolation, post-op complications, neonatal problems, postpartum psychosis, depression, domestic abuse...' She fixed him with her gaze. 'The list goes on and on.'

He didn't want to smile. He should be annoyed. This woman was practically putting him in his place. But he couldn't help but feel he might have deserved it.

He wondered how on earth she'd ended up here. She'd already mentioned a daughter. And she clearly wasn't wearing a wedding ring. It was absolutely none of his business. But Jacob Layton's curiosity was definitely sparked. He liked this feisty midwife.

He spoke steadily. 'That certainly seems like enough experience. So what made you come down to Cambridge? It's a long way from Scotland.'

She didn't even stop to think. Her eyes were still flashing. Bonnie Reid was on a roll. 'That's the thing about finding your husband in bed with your best friend—it makes you want to get as far away as possible.'

Silence.

You could have heard a proverbial pin drop. Bonnie felt the colour rush to her cheeks and she lifted her hand to her mouth. Oh, no. Why on earth would she say something like that out loud?

It was that darn man. Jacob Layton. It wasn't bad enough that the handsomest man on the planet had watched her walking down the corridor as if he were undressing her with his eyes. Then he'd started talking to her and everything he'd said had put her back up. Now she'd lost her rag with him. Hardly the best start in a new job.

But Bonnie Reid didn't take any prisoners. In this life, she meant to start the way she was going to continue. The part of her life where she put up with bad behaviour, indifference and rudeness was over.

Maybe it was the fact he was so good-looking that was unnerving her. If she got any closer she was sure she'd see gold flecks in those intense green eyes. Or maybe it was the fact that no man had even flickered on her radar since she'd walked away from her ex. Certainly not a brown-haired, green-eyed Hollywood-style hunk.

Her insides were cringing. She couldn't believe what she'd just said. And it was clear from the faces around her that no one else could either.

But what made it all the more excruciating was the fact that the edges of Jacob Layton's mouth seemed to be turning upwards.

He was laughing at her.

'Please come with me,' he said sharply and walked over, ushering her towards an office door with Head Obstetrician emblazoned across it, and away from the gaping mouths.

He closed the door firmly behind them and walked around his desk. 'Take a seat.' His voice was firm and she felt a wave of panic sweep over her.

She hadn't even officially started—was she about to be fired? 'I'm sorry. I've no idea where that came from.'

Her stomach did a little flip-flop. It didn't matter. It really didn't matter but she'd just made a fool of herself in front of the resident hunk and her new boss. She'd just told him that her husband had cheated on her. It was hardly a placard that she wanted to wave above her head. She might as well be holding a sign saying 'I'm plain and boring in bed'.

The humiliation burned her cheeks. Right now she wanted to crawl into a hole.

He fixed on her with those green eyes and she felt her skin prickle under her thin scrubs. At times like this she longed for her thicker white tunic and navy trousers. But scrubs were the order of the day in most labour wards.

He pointed to the chair again. 'Sit down.'

Her feet were shuffling nervously on the carpet and she couldn't stop wringing her hands together. Sitting down seemed quite claustrophobic. Particularly with Jacob sitting at the other side of the desk and the door closed behind them.

'Don't ever speak to me like that again in front of my colleagues.' The words were out before she could stop them. And she wasn't finished. 'It was unprofessional. If you want to question my clinical capabilities take it up with me privately, or take it up with the director of midwives who employed me.' She waved her hand. 'On second thoughts, why don't you actually wait until you've worked with me, *before* you question my clinical capabilities?' She stuck her hands on her hips. 'And maybe I'll wait until then to question yours.'

Too much. It was too much. Even she knew that. The shocked expression on his face almost made her want to open the door and run back down the corridor.

Definitely not her best start.

She took a deep breath and sat down. 'Look—' she started but Jacob lifted his hand.

She froze mid-sentence. This was the way she always got when she was nervous. Her mouth started running away with her, a prime example being what had happened outside.

Jacob ran his hand through his hair. It struck her as an odd act. Usually a sign of someone being tired or frustrated. Jacob Layton didn't strike her as any of those things.

He lifted his eyes to meet hers. 'You're right. I shouldn't have questioned your capabilities. But let's start with the basics. Bonnie, I would have preferred it if you could have been here at nine this morning. It would have made our meeting a little easier. Is timing going to be an issue for you?'

She shook her head quickly, wondering if she should be offended by the question. 'No. Not at all. This morning was a one-off.'

He gave the tiniest nod. 'I appreciate you just arrived last night, and that you were asked to start at short notice.' His brow furrowed a little. 'Do you have adequate arrangements in place for your daughter?'

She straightened her shoulders. He was putting her on edge again. Dr Handsome just seemed to rub her up the wrong way. 'I hope so. I have a friend who is a registered childminder. She's agreed to take Freya in the mornings and after school.'

'What about weekends and night shifts?'

Bonnie felt herself pull back a little. 'I was told there was no requirement for night shifts—that you had permanent night shift staff here?' The statement had turned into a question. She had the mildest feeling of panic.

A wave of recognition flickered across his face. 'What about shift work? Will that cause you a problem?

Now he was really getting her back up. She couldn't fathom this guy out at all. One minute he was fiercely professional, the next he looked amused by her. As for the sparks that had shot up her arm when they'd touched...

She'd already snapped at this guy once. She didn't want to do it again. It wasn't his fault she was tired. It wasn't his fault that the journey from Scotland had taken much more out of her and Freya than she'd really expected. It wasn't his fault Freya had been upset this morning, or that the motel room was totally inappropriate for them both. None of this was his fault.

She wanted to respect her boss and get on well with him. He was a bit grumpy, but she'd met worse, and she was sure she could knock it out of him. She'd already embarrassed herself once in front of her boss. It was time for a new tack.

She met his gaze straight on. 'Jacob, I don't think you're actually allowed to ask me questions like that.'

'Aren't I?' He sat back quickly and frowned.

She held up her hands. 'Would you ask a guy these questions?' She was so aware it was all about the tone here. It was a serious subject, but she was quite sure he wasn't even aware of what he was doing. 'What if I asked you, right now, about childcare arrangements for any kids you might have? Would that seem appropriate to you?'

The recognition dawned quickly on his face. 'Well... no.' He put his head in his hands for a second and shook it. When he pulled his head back up he had a sorry smile on his face and shrugged his shoulders. 'Sorry.'

She gave a little nod of her head. 'No problem.'

She heard him suck in a breath and his shoulders relaxed a little. 'I do have a good reason for asking you.'

She raised her eyebrows. 'You do?'

He nodded slowly. 'I do.' He was being serious now. 'Valerie Glencross, the director of midwifery, suggested we should offer you a promoted post.'

Bonnie sat bolt upright in her chair. It was the last thing she'd expected to hear. 'She did?'

His gaze connected with hers. 'She did.' For a second it felt as if time had frozen. She was looking into the brightest pair of green eyes she'd ever seen. She'd been right. He had little gold flecks in his irises. It made them sparkle. It was making her hold her breath as she realised exactly what kind of an effect they were having on her.

'She did,' he reiterated. 'It seems your CV had already

impressed her. I'm guessing that your telephone interview with her went well. She wanted me to meet you and ask if you'd consider being Ward Sister on a temporary basis.'

'Me?' Bonnie was more than a little surprised. 'But you must have senior staff working here already. Wouldn't it make more sense to have someone take charge who is familiar with the set-up?'

He gave a little laugh. 'You would think so. Our senior staff are excellent. But none of them have the talent of organisation. Valerie said that before you were a community midwife you were a ward sister. I think she thought it would be good to have a new broom, so to speak. Someone who didn't have any preconceived ideas about CRMU and could bring some fresh ideas about how things should run.' He gave a little sigh. 'Our ward sister Abby has been gone less than two weeks and it's chaos out there. She left sooner than expected and we obviously didn't appreciate just how much she kept on top of things.' He gave his head a little shake. 'I'm feeling bad. I'm wondering if the stress of the ward was a factor in her pre-eclampsia.'

'Is she okay?' It was the first thing that sprang to mind.

He gave a quick nod and Bonnie shot him a smile. 'In that case, you're not making it sound like my dream job. Shouldn't you be giving me the hard sell? And after our first meeting—do you really want to offer it to me at all?' Jacob Layton wasn't good at this. He was being too honest.

He groaned again and sat straighter, giving her a grin that sent tingles to her toes. 'Let me start again. Bonnie Reid—from your extensive experience on your CV we've decided you would be a great addition to our team. You'll know the reputation of Cambridge Royal Maternity Unit.

We employ the best obstetricians and midwives and are known as a centre of medical excellence. We have links with Cambridge University and are pioneers in the development and research of many groundbreaking medical techniques. We have a great bunch of staff working in the labour delivery suite. We just need someone who can bring some new organisational skills to the ward.' He leaned across the table towards her. 'How's that for the hard sell?'

She couldn't pull her eyes away from his. He was closer to her than ever before. She could see every strand of his dark brown hair. See the tiny lines around his eyes. And exactly just how straight and white his teeth were.

He nodded towards her. 'And yes, I do want to offer it to you. You're the first person to answer back in about five years.'

Boy, he was handsome. But there was something else. Something so much more than just good looks. Beneath the flecks of gold in his eyes she could see another part of Jacob Layton. There was so much more there than a handsome but grumpy obstetrician. He seemed the single-minded, career-driven type. But what lay beneath the driven exterior?

She returned his smile. 'That was much better.'

He relaxed back in his chair and she was almost sorry she'd replied. 'Thank goodness.' He was so much nicer like this. Why did he act so grumpy around the staff?

She took a deep breath. 'I want this to work. I want this to work for me and for Freya—my little girl. This is a fresh start. I want to leave everything else behind us.' She rolled her eyes and gave her head a little shake. 'And I definitely want to leave men behind. I just want to focus on my new job and getting me and my daughter settled.'

Jacob gave a little nod of acknowledgement as he

tapped his fingers on the desk. 'The reason I asked about your childcare arrangements—if you're working as ward sister we'd generally expect you to work nine to five. You'd only occasionally be expected to work late shifts if there were staffing issues, and join part of the hospital on-call rota to do weekends.'

Bonnie frowned. 'How does that work?'

'All of our ward sisters take turns in covering weekends. You're not actually there as a member of the team that weekend. You're covering the management for the whole hospital. Sorting out staffing problems, dealing with any difficult cases or issues across the whole of maternity. It usually works out once every nine weeks.'

Bonnie nodded. 'That's understandable. This would make things much easier with my childcare arrangements. Freya will be much happier if I'm working more or less regular hours. I'll get to put her to bed most nights. And, as I've mentioned, Lynn will happily take Freya every weekday before and after school, and for the occasional late night or weekend.' She gave a visible sigh of relief. 'I'm happy to do the job—in fact, I'm really excited to be asked.'

He seemed relieved. 'So you'll take the job?' His voice went up a little, as if he was still a bit anxious she might turn down this fabulous opportunity.

She stood up and held out her hand towards him. 'Of course I will. I'm a little nervous but am sure in a few days it will feel like I've been here for weeks. That's always the way of it, isn't it?'

He smiled again; this time the relief was definitely reaching right up into his eyes. His hand grasped hers. There it was again.

She hadn't been mistaken first time around. Coming into contact with Jacob Layton's hand was doing strange things to her skin receptors—currently it was the dance of a thousand butterflies. Just as well she'd made it clear she was a man-free zone.

'Perfect. I'll let Valerie know you've accepted. She'll arrange for a new contract.' He held open the door for her. 'Now, let's go and tell the staff.'

Her stomach did another little flip-flop as she walked through, but she couldn't work out if that was the thought of telling her new peers about her role, or from the burn coming from Jacob's hand at the small of her back.

One thing was for sure—CRMU was going to be interesting.

CHAPTER TWO

JACOB HADN'T BEEN WRONG. The labour suite was in chaos. And it was all basics.

Bonnie grabbed a ward clerk and made some immediate requests about sorting out case notes, filing things appropriately and keeping the boards up to date. Then she asked for new lists of contact numbers. The one she found on the wall was obviously out of date and, with doctors changing every six months, she didn't want any problems with pagers in case of emergency.

She spent the next two hours working with various members of staff and patients. After a few hours she was confident in the clinical capabilities of the staff that were on duty. They all wanted to do their jobs and work with patients. They just didn't want to bother with 'ward' stuff. Ordering, stocking, rotas, outpatient appointments, pharmacy prescriptions. It quickly became apparent that her predecessor had dealt with all these things and her quick departure meant there had been no handover.

Bonnie gave a sigh. She'd like to spend all day working with patients too—but that wasn't the way a ward was run. She started making a 'to do' list that she'd have to work her way through.

The other issue was the phones. They rang constantly—often with no one answering. First thing tomorrow she was going to ask about a regular ward clerk for the unit. Just as she finished making a few notes about the off-duty rota the phone rang again.

'CRMU, Bonnie Reid, can I help you?'

'Ambulance Control. We need a team on-site at a crash on one of the motorway slip roads. We have a trapped, unconscious pregnant woman. She's reported to be thirty-four weeks. Ambulance is on its way to pick you up.'

Bonnie put down the phone. First day on the job. You had to be joking. She automatically dialled the page for the on-call obstetrician. Most big maternity units had supplies for emergencies like these. It was just a pity she hadn't had a chance to find out where they were.

A few seconds later Jacob appeared from his office just as Bonnie was relaying the message to one of the senior midwives. He was holding his page. 'What have we got?'

She handed over the piece of paper she'd scribbled on. Jacob gestured towards her. 'Follow me. Equipment is in here. Grab a jacket and a bag.' He turned to face her. 'You are coming, aren't you?'

She hesitated for only the briefest of seconds. 'If you want me to.'

No. I'm terrified. This sounds like an initiation of fire. It's my first day, I've just agreed to act as temporary sister in one of the most prestigious maternity units in the country and now you want me to be part of the emergency response team.

He acted as if he did this every day, grabbing a jacket with 'Doctor' emblazoned across the back and handing her the one with 'Midwife'. He shot her a smile as he helped her lift the emergency pack onto her shoulders. 'Let's go. Leave instructions with Miriam, the senior midwife. She'll deal with the calls until we get back.'

He walked away, his long strides crossing the corridor quickly, only stopping to wheel a portable incubator to the door.

She could feel the wave of panic lapping around her ankles. There was no way she could let it go any further. She started repeating in her head the list of emergencies that she'd dealt with on her own as a community midwife. She could do this. She could.

Miriam gave her a sympathetic nod as she handed over a few instructions. 'I'm so glad it's you and not me,' she murmured under her breath.

'What do you mean?'

Miriam rolled her eyes. 'If you think Dan Daring is harsh on the ward, you should see him at a roadside emergency. The patients love him. The rest of the staff need counselling by the time he's done.'

'Let's go, Bonnie!' The shout made her jump and she hurried to the exit and into the back of the waiting ambulance. As soon as the doors closed and the sirens switched on they were on their way.

Sitting in the back of the ambulance was more than a little bumpy. She only just managed to avoid practically bouncing onto Jacob's lap. But he barely noticed. He was holding on to the strap in the back with his eyes fixed on the road ahead.

'Any more news?'

One of the paramedics turned around. 'All bad. We've just had a report that they think her membranes might have ruptured. She's still unconscious and trapped. They're panicking. They think she's gone into labour.' He glanced at the clock. 'We'll be there in five minutes.'

Bonnie sucked in a breath. A thousand different potential diagnoses were flying through her head. From Jacob's serious expression he was thinking the same.

When they screeched to a halt Jacob didn't wait, he just flung open the doors, grabbed the bag and started running.

The first thing that struck her was the smell. Fire, burning metal, petrol and a whole lot more. There were four ambulances already on-site. A few casualties were sitting on the edge of the road. Two children with blood on their faces, a man cradling his arm and an older woman who looked completely shell-shocked. Police had cordoned off part of the motorway but the speed and noise of the cars still passing by was unnerving. Rubbernecking. That was what most of the passing cars were doing. Any minute now there would be another accident on the other side of the motorway. She shuddered and jumped out of the back of the ambulance, trying to spot Jacob's bright green jacket in amongst the melee of emergency people.

'Over here.' A policeman gestured her towards an up-ended car. She stepped around the pieces of car debris that littered the road. Somewhere, she could hear someone crying. The wails cutting through the rest of the sounds. It was horrible. It was unnerving.

She landed on her knees next to the upturned car. The only thing she could currently see of Jacob was the soles of his feet. His whole body was inside the car, his feet sticking out through the broken passenger-side window. 'Do you need anything?' she shouted through the gap.

She adjusted her position to get a better view. Inside the car a pregnant woman was trapped upside down, held precariously in position by her seat belt. It was obvious she was still unconscious, an oxygen mask to her face and a collar around her neck. Jacob was pushing back her coat and gently easing her stretched top over her abdomen. Bonnie didn't wait for instructions. She fished out a stethoscope and a foetal monitor and stuck her hand through a gap in the broken window where Jacob could grab them.

Even from here she could see the damp patch between the woman's trousers. It could be two things. It could be urine or it could be amniotic fluid. She was just praying it wasn't blood. She didn't even want to consider that— not under these conditions.

After a few minutes of wrestling around Jacob finally spoke. 'I've got a heartbeat—albeit a little quick. But I've just felt her contracting and there's absolutely no way to do any kind of examination.'

He shook his head as Bonnie tried to hand him the nitrazine strips. The best they could do in this situation was rub one against her damp clothes. 'There's no point checking. I'm fairly sure her membranes have ruptured. We need to get her out of here now. She's at risk of uterine or placental rupture. There's no way I'm delivering this baby upside down.'

Bonnie stood up and shouted over to the fire and rescue colleagues. 'We need to get this woman out. She's about to deliver. Can we have some assistance?'

One of them ran over. 'Sorry, got tied up trying to lift a car off someone's chest.'

Bonnie gulped. It was chaos all around them and even though the road seemed full of emergency staff, there probably still wasn't enough.

The fire-and-rescue guy pointed at the collar. 'She was conscious for only a few seconds after we arrived and had no feeling in her legs. That's why the collar's in place. The trauma doc said not to move her. He was waiting for you to arrive.'

She nodded. 'Well, tell the trauma doc we're here and

she's in labour. We need assistance to move her as safely as possible now. Can you get us a backboard?'

She pushed her way around the other side of the car. The driver's door was wedged up against a van that was on its side. It was a struggle to push her arms through and try and wind a blood-pressure cuff around the lady's arm. 'Do we have a name?' she shouted to Jacob.

'Holly Burns.'

She pressed the button on the machine. Now she'd squeezed around the other side she could see him a little easier. There were deep furrows along his brow; he was clearly worried about this patient and so was she.

'BP's low,' she said quickly as the result displayed.

A number of the fire-and-rescue crew had collected around them, all talking in low voices. 'Doc, we're going to have to move the car. We need to cut the patient free and we can't do it while the van's in place. You'll need to come out.'

Jacob didn't hesitate. 'I'm going nowhere. This mother and her baby need monitoring every second. Move the car with me in it.'

One of them stepped forwards as Bonnie wriggled out from the other side. She could see clearly why they would need to separate the vehicles. There was no way they could get Holly out on a backboard otherwise. If she had spinal damage they had to do everything possible to try to minimise the movement.

She shook her head and touched the fire-and-rescue chief's arm. 'Don't waste your time arguing with him. He won't change his mind and it'll just get ugly. This woman could deliver very soon and her position makes it dangerous for her life and her baby's.'

She was quite sure this went against every health and safety check imaginable. But she'd seen fire and rescue, paramedic and police services do similar things before. They all made the patient their priority.

She stood back as equipment was positioned and blankets shoved inside the car as Jacob was told to brace himself and his patient.

The car and van were wedged tightly together. The sound of metal ripping apart made her wince. Nothing about this was delicate. Both the car and van were juddering, wheels spinning in the air. It seemed to take for ever before they were finally yanked apart and the fire-and-rescue crew moved in with their cutting equipment.

It only took seconds for them to cut the side from the car. One of the other trauma doctors appeared with the backboard and had a quick confab with Jacob inside about the best way to cut Holly free from her seat belt and support her spine. It was a delicate operation. Twelve pairs of hands ended up all around her, ready to ease her gently onto the spinal board as the seat belt was cut. 'Hold it,' said Jacob abruptly. 'She's having another contraction. We'll have to wait a few seconds for it to pass.'

Bonnie swallowed anxiously. Jacob still had the foetal monitor on Holly's swollen abdomen. She could see the contraction clearly. As an experienced midwife she knew Holly wasn't in the early stages of labour, even though she was upside down. A thought flicked through her mind—had Holly already been in labour and on her way to the hospital before the crash? Or was this a trauma-induced labour brought on by the crash? One thing was for sure: as soon as they got Holly into the ambulance, they'd better be prepared for a delivery.

As the seat belt was cut and Holly slid onto the backboard Bonnie glanced around. 'Does anyone know about next of kin?' she shouted. They were just about to take

Holly away from the accident site. There hadn't been a chance to get all the information they needed.

One of the policemen appeared at her elbow. 'We've sent someone to contact her husband. Are you taking her to CRMU?'

Bonnie nodded. 'Can you give me her husband's name and contact details?'

He nodded and scribbled in his notebook, ripping out the page and handing it to her. By the time she turned around Holly was already being loaded onto the ambulance.

Jacob was ruthlessly efficient. The other trauma doctor secured Holly's head and neck, checking her airway before he left. He was part of the general team from Cambridge Royal. 'I have to accompany another patient back with a flail chest. I'll send an orthopod around to the maternity unit.' Jacob gave him the briefest nod as he attached the monitoring equipment. Bonnie barely got inside as the doors slammed shut and the ambulance started off at breakneck speed.

'There's another contraction coming,' she said as she finished attaching the BP cuff and heart monitor. She helped him slide off Holly's underwear and covered her abdomen with a blanket.

Jacob's frown deepened. 'She's crowning. This baby is coming out any minute.'

Bonnie turned towards the portable incubator, struggling to stay on her feet as the ambulance rocked from side to side. There had to be rules about this. She was sure they were supposed to be strapped in. But this baby wasn't waiting for anyone, and what use would two health professionals be at her head or at her side, while a baby slipped out?

She was doing rapid calculations in her head. 'She's

thirty-four weeks. That's not too early. Hopefully the baby won't have any breathing difficulties.' She switched on the monitoring equipment in the incubator, ensuring it was warm and the oxygen was ready.

It was difficult to take up position in the swaying ambulance. She could only try and lift Holly's nearest leg, holding it in position to allow Jacob easier access to the presenting head.

She gulped. 'She's missing out on the birth of her baby.' She blinked back tears. 'I hope she doesn't miss out on anything else.'

This was awful. Her first delivery for CRMU with a mother that she didn't even know would wake up. Why was she still unconscious? The trauma doctor had only given her a quick once-over. There hadn't been time for anything else. A Glasgow Coma Scale chart dangled from a clipboard. As each contraction gripped there were facial twinges—as if she were reacting to some element of the labour pain. Reaction to pain was a crucial part of the head injury assessment. And she was breathing spontaneously. Bonnie tried to focus on the positives. She would hate to think this mother would never get to hold her new baby.

As another contraction gripped Holly's stomach the head delivered. Jacob had a quick check around the baby's neck for any sign of a cord. He glanced quickly in Bonnie's direction. 'No cord. Presentation is good.' He gave an audible sigh of relief. 'Thank goodness.'

One minute later the baby slid into his hands and he quickly handed it over to Bonnie.

A little girl. Just like Freya. A fist squeezed around her heart. She'd heard Freya's first cries, felt her first little breaths against her chest. Holly was missing all of this.

She quickly gave the pale little baby a rub, stimulating her first noisy breath, followed by some sharp cries. She gave Jacob a quick smile before wrapping the baby in the warming blanket and doing a quick assessment. 'APGAR six,' she said as she finished.

It was a little low, but would likely come up before the second check in five minutes. It was certainly better than she'd initially hoped for.

She looked up; they were pulling up in front of the emergency entrance at the maternity unit. Three other staff were waiting for them.

Jacob moved into position as the doors opened and helped lift the incubator down. 'Take her to the nursery and get a paed doc to check her over.'

Bonnie gave a brief nod and headed down the corridor with one of the nursery midwives by her side. The handover was quick. The little girl was pinking up now and was letting everyone know she wasn't entirely happy with her entrance to the world.

By the time Bonnie got back to the labour suite, Jacob was consulting with the orthopaedic doctor who'd come over from the main hospital. Holly's notes had appeared at the desk. Thankfully, she had no significant medical history and her pregnancy seemed to have gone well. Bonnie could see from the whiteboard that Miriam, the senior midwife, was with her.

'Has she woken up yet?' She was having trouble getting her head around the fact that Holly had delivered a baby without being conscious. 'In ten years of midwifery I've never seen a woman labour while unconscious.' She blinked back the tears that threatened to spill over. 'Does she have some kind of head injury?'

The orthopaedic doctor glanced at Jacob, then leaned over and touched Bonnie's arm. 'It actually might not be as bad as first thought. She almost certainly has a head injury but her Glasgow Coma Scale responses are im-proving. I suspect Holly's in spinal shock from injuries sustained in the crash. She wouldn't have felt the inten-sity of the labour pains even though her body naturally delivered. Jacob and I were just discussing the fact that we think she might actually have been in labour prior to the accident. We've checked the ward call log. She hadn't called into the labour suite and she didn't have any bags in her car. We're wondering if she was going home to collect her things.'

Bonnie nodded. She could only remember a few things about spinal shock from her general nurse training. It was usually temporary but could cause loss of sensation and feeling. It certainly sounded better than some of the things she'd been imagining.

Jacob's voice cut across her thoughts. 'I take it the lit-tle girl is okay?' He was glaring and it took her a couple of seconds to realise it wasn't at her—well, not entirely. His eyes were fixed on the orthopaedic doctor's hand, which was still on Bonnie's arm.

Was Jacob this territorial around all his staff?

She gave a nod to the orthopod and walked behind the desk to pick up some paper notes. 'Baby Burns is doing fine. APGAR was eight at five minutes. The paediatri-cian was checking her as I left.' She waved the notes at Jacob. 'I'm just going to write up some midwifery notes for what happened out there. I'll get the clerk to put Holly and baby Burns into the hospital admission system.'

There was a bang at the bottom of the corridor as the doors were flung open. Both Bonnie and Jacob jumped to their feet. It wasn't entirely unusual for people to enter the labour suite in a rush. This time, though, there was no pregnant woman—just an extremely anxious man.

'My wife, Holly, is she here? They said there was a car accident. What happened? Is she okay? Is the baby okay?'

Jacob and the orthopaedic doctor exchanged glances. Jacob gestured towards his office. 'Mr Burns, why don't you come into my office and I'll let you know what has happened?'

The man's face paled even more and he wobbled. 'Are they dead?'

Jacob quickly reassured him. 'No, no, they're not dead. And you can see them both. Let's just have a chat first.' He turned to the orthopaedic doctor. 'Dr Connelly, will you join us, please?'

But the man's feet were welded to the floor. His eyes widened. 'Both? The baby is here?'

Bonnie walked over, putting her hand on his arm. 'You have a lovely daughter. I'll take you to see her once you've spoken to the doctors.' She helped usher him into the office and, once he was inside, closed the door behind him and left them to it.

'Debbie' The labour suite domestic was working in the kitchen. 'Would you mind taking a pot of tea into Dr Layton's office? I think the man he's talking to will need some.'

Debbie gave a little laugh. 'Tea, for Jacob? You've got to be joking. The guy drinks his coffee with three spoonfuls.' She shook her head. 'You'll soon learn he usually has a cup from the café across the street welded to his hand. Don't worry. I'll sort it out.'

For the rest of the day Bonnie's feet barely touched the ground. She finished her notes, took over from Miriam for a while, then took Mr Burns along to see his new daughter.

Holly had gradually started to come round. Things were complicated. Midwives really shouldn't be dealing with a patient with a head injury. But Holly had a few other complications with the delivery of her placenta. She really wasn't suitable to be on a general ward either. After some careful calls and juggling, Bonnie finally managed to make sure that either a midwife who was also trained as a general nurse was looking after her, or that an extra nurse be called over from the brief intervention unit. After the first twenty-four hours she'd need to be reassessed and other arrangements made.

By the time Jacob came to find her she'd no idea where the time had gone. Opening one store cupboard to have most of its contents fall on her head, followed by finding some out-of-date drugs in one of the cupboards was making her organisational skills go into overload. She wouldn't be able to sleep tonight with the 'to do' lists she currently had stored in her head.

'Just thought I should check how you are.'

She picked her way back through the untidy contents of the store cupboard. 'I'm fine, thanks.' She glanced at her watch. 'Is that the time already? The childminder will wonder where I am.'

She let out a groan. 'Darn it. I haven't found us somewhere else to stay.'

'What do you mean? You don't know where you are staying?'

Bonnie sucked in a deep breath. 'That's the thing about agreeing to start at short notice. I haven't managed to find somewhere to rent. I haven't even had a chance to view anywhere. The motel I booked is awful. We got in last night and it's damp and I'm pretty sure there are signs of mildew. It's going to play havoc with Freya's asthma. I need to find somewhere else as soon as I can. I had a quick look online last night and most places aren't available for rent until after Christmas. I've obviously come at the wrong time of year.' She kept shaking her head. She sighed and leaned against the doorjamb. 'I need to find somewhere quick. I just assumed that I'd be able to find somewhere without any problem. It is a city, after all.'

Accommodation wasn't something Jacob had even considered for their new start. As a mother she wouldn't have the option of staying in the hospital flats. They were only designed for singles.

He shook his head. 'Cambridge isn't like most cities. We don't have a huge turnover except when the university year starts. Most students find accommodation and stay in it for four full years.'

She shrugged. 'I'll just need to try a bit harder, I guess. More importantly I'll need to get a car. Relying on public transport is a bit of a nightmare. The sooner I get home to Freya, the better.'

He spoke before he thought. 'I'll give you a lift home.'

She blinked. The shock on her face was apparent. Had he really been that unfriendly to her earlier?

'You don't have to do that.'

'I know. But I will. You've had a bit of a baptism of fire today. I know you want to get home to Freya and the buses will be busy this time of day.' He shrugged. 'It's only five minutes out of my way. We'll go in ten minutes.'

The phone rang further along the ward and Hope Sanders, one of the other midwives, stuck her head out of one of the rooms. 'Jacob? Can you come and take this call?'

He didn't even give her a chance to respond before he walked swiftly along the corridor. He was impressed. Bonnie was doing a good job. He hadn't even given a thought to where she might be staying. If she was worried about that—would she be able to focus on her work?

Hope handed him the phone. 'It's Sean Anderson. He wants to know if you can help in Theatre tomorrow.'

The call only took a few minutes. Jacob liked Sean, the new Australian obstetrician, and he was happy to scrub in on a complicated case. Hope waited for him to finish the call, her arms folded across her chest, leaning on the door.

'What?' he asked as he replaced the receiver.

'How are you?' she asked steadily.

He felt himself flinch. Hope was one of the few people he classed as a friend. She knew exactly what kind of year he'd had. 'I'm fine.'

She nodded slowly. There was no way he'd get away with that kind of answer with Hope. 'When do you get your test results?'

He shifted uncomfortably on his feet. He hated being put on the spot. 'A few weeks.'

'And you're feeling well? Anything I can do?'

He shook his head and picked up some paperwork from his desk. 'I'm fine, Hope. There's no need to fuss.'

She gave him a tight smile. Hope was never bothered by his short answers or occasionally sharp tongue. She just ignored it and asked the questions she wanted to ask.

'Did you reconsider my suggestion?'

'What one?' Hope made lots of suggestions. He should socialise more. He should do less hours at work. He should eat better. He should be more pleasant at work.

She raised her eyebrows. 'About renting out one of your rooms?' Oh. That one. Her latest suggestion was a bid to encapsulate all her suggestions: it would force him to socialise, he might work less if he had someone to go home to, someone who could cook, maybe.

'Haven't had a chance.' He walked from behind the desk and gave her a cheeky wink. 'Been too busy at work.'

'Jacob…' Her voice tailed after him but he was already halfway down the corridor. Hope was about to go into interrogator mode. He could sense it. It was time to make a sharp exit.

Bonnie was just finishing at the desk and he welcomed the distraction. If Hope saw him talking to another woman she was bound to leave him alone.

'Good first day?' he asked.

Bonnie blinked. 'It's not over yet. Come with me a second.'

She took another quick glance over her shoulder at the bustling labour suite. *Her* bustling labour suite. She hadn't even started to make her mark here. They walked down the corridor together.

So many things needed organising to make the place run more efficiently. Once she had things running the way she liked and she knew the staff a little better she'd start to delegate some tasks. All of the staff she'd met today seemed fine. No one had even mentioned what they'd overheard this morning, but she was sure—by the time she came on shift tomorrow—all members of staff would know about it. That was the thing about hospitals. Nothing was kept secret for long.

She'd met seven midwives, two doctors and one other consultant who all seemed good at their jobs. The ancillary staff seemed great too. CRMU's reputation appeared to be well founded. All the labour suite needed was its wheels oiled a little to help it run more smoothly.

She smiled. First day. After a bumpy start with Freya, and with Jacob, things appeared to be looking up. Good staff. A temporary promotion. Three healthy babies delivered while she was on shift. And another delivered in the back of an ambulance with a mother who appeared to be on the road to recovery.

Jacob had surprised her most with his offer of a ride home. At their first meeting he'd appeared a little detached. But at times today his mouth had betrayed him by turning up at the edges. There was a sense of humour in there somewhere. She'd just have to find a big spade to dig it out.

She pushed open the doors at the end of the ward and walked along to one of the side rooms between her ward and the special-care nursery. Both of them looked through the window. Holly had opened her eyes and was talking to one of the specialist midwives assigned to her. Her husband sat by her side holding the baby in his arms. Another midwife from the special-care nursery was there with the incubator. It was obvious this was the first time she'd got to see her baby.

The whole scene sent a warm glow around Bonnie's body. Coming here was the best decision she'd ever made.

She met Jacob's emerald gaze. There was a gleam in his eye. He knew exactly what kind of day she'd had. She kept her face straight. 'No. It's not been a good day.'

He raised his eyebrows and she broke into a beaming smile. 'It was a *great* day. I think I'm going to like Cambridge Maternity.'

CHAPTER THREE

JACOB TAPPED HIS fingers on the wheel of the car while he waited for Bonnie. He'd already had a few curious stares from members of staff who obviously wondered who he was waiting on. Bonnie appeared two minutes later and jumped in the car next to him. 'Sorry, just getting changed and sorting out a locker before we left.' She gave him directions to the childminder's house and looked around with a smile on her face.

'I didn't take you for a four-by-four guy. I thought you'd have something sleeker, more sporty.'

He raised his eyebrows. 'Really? Why on earth did you think that?'

She laughed. 'You've got that "I drive a flash car" look about you. Wouldn't have thought there'd be much call for a four-by-four in the city. I've been surprised by how many I've seen.'

'Haven't you heard? It's the latest fashion craze and I'm just following the crowd.'

She shook her head. 'Yeah, yeah. Somehow I get the distinct impression you've never been a crowd follower.'

He tried to hide his smile. 'I'm shocked. We've only just met and you're trying to tell me I'm not a people pleaser.'

She started laughing again. 'Seriously? You were a bit

grumpy this morning. The staff seem quite intimidated by you. Are you always like that?'

'You were late. That's why I was grumpy.' It was the best excuse he could give. The truth was he'd spent the last fourteen months being grumpy—and only a few select people knew why. Jacob had always been a completely hands-on kind of doctor. Some physicians who were Head of Department reduced their clinical time by a large amount. He'd never been that kind of doctor but had been grateful to use his position as an excuse for his lack of patient contact at times over the past fourteen months. That was the thing about some types of chemotherapy—at certain times in the cycle, patient contact just wasn't appropriate. Particularly when you had to deal with pregnant women and neonates—two of the most vulnerable groups around. Grumpy probably didn't even come close to covering his temperament and frustration these last fourteen months.

She shook her head as they turned into the childminder's street. 'I think you were grumpy long before I was late. I need to know these things. I need to know if staff won't want to approach you about things. I need to know the dynamics of the labour suite.'

He liked her already. She was astute. It wouldn't be easy to pull the wool over her eyes—exactly what he should want from the sister of his labour suite. He just wished she weren't using her astuteness on him.

'You haven't mentioned what happens with the special clients. Do I get involved with those?'

He raised his eyebrows. 'The special clients?'

She smiled. 'Cambridge Royal is known for attracting the rich and famous. I haven't had a chance to look over the plans for the general hospital. What happens if we get someone who wants a private delivery? It wouldn't seem safe to have them in another area.'

He was impressed. She'd obviously done a lot of background reading. 'You're right. It wouldn't be safe. It isn't public knowledge but there are six private rooms just outside the doors to the labour suite, only a few minutes from Theatre. We don't want anyone to know where our private patients are.'

She gave a little nod of her head. 'Makes sense. Privacy, that's what people want. Isn't it? I guess we'll need to talk about the midwifery staffing for those rooms.'

There was something so strange about all this. Everything about being around Bonnie made him feel out of sorts. He had looked at her CV and hadn't understood at all why Valerie Glencross had thought she would be a suitable replacement for their ward sister. Then she'd been late.

But from the second her eyes had sparked and she'd given him a dressing-down in front of the staff he'd liked her. She was different. She'd proved more than competent at the roadside delivery. She was asking all the right questions about the ward and she was making all the right observations. Bonnie Reid was proving to be the most interesting woman he'd come across in a while.

She opened the car door as they pulled up outside the childminder's. 'I'll only be two minutes, I promise, and Lynn will be able to give me a car seat for Freya. That's the beauty of having a friend who is a childminder. She has a garage full of these things.'

Car seat. It hadn't even crossed his mind. That was how far out of the loop he was when it came to children. He tried not to focus on her well-fitting jeans as she ran up the path towards the door with her auburn hair bouncing behind her.

What kind of crazy fool cheated on a woman like Bonnie? The guy must have rocks in his head. Jacob had never realised quite how much he liked that colour of hair.

He watched as she ran back down the path holding the hand of a little girl. She was like an identikit of her mother. Same colour hair and pale skin. It only took Bonnie a minute to arrange the car seat and strap her little girl into place. She was obviously a dab hand at these things.

'Who are you?' The voice came from the back seat.

The little pair of curious blue eyes was fixed on his in the mirror. She had a little furrow across her brow. It was like a staring contest. A Mexican stand-off. And Jacob had a feeling he was going to lose.

Bonnie answered as she climbed back in the car. 'This is Mummy's friend from work. His name is Jacob. He's going to give us a lift back to the motel.'

He glanced in the rear-view mirror in time to see her shrink back into her seat a little. Was he really that scary? Bonnie had already mentioned the staff might find him unapproachable. He'd never really given it much thought.

'Hmm…' came the voice from the back of the car. She really didn't seem too sure about it. Bonnie gave him directions to the motel and he flinched when it came into view. If this was the outside—what was the inside like?

'Do you need a hand?'

'No,' she said too quickly, then her voice wavered. 'Actually, could you give me a hand carrying the car seat in?' She jumped out and unstrapped Freya, leading the way inside.

He followed them in, waiting patiently while she unlocked the door of her room. The first thing that hit him was the smell of damp. The really obvious smell of damp. He winced. How on earth did the motel owner think this was acceptable?

He looked around. 'This will play havoc with Freya's asthma.' The words came out before he really thought about it.

Bonnie sucked in a deep breath and licked her lips. There was a sheen across her eyes, as if she was holding back tears.

She'd already told him how much this bothered her. But now, seeing it with his own eyes, he understood.

Bonnie's pretty face was marred by a frown. He liked her. He hardly knew her but he liked her already. What was more she obviously had the skills that the labour suite badly needed right now.

And after what he'd seen today? He didn't want to lose her from CRMU.

His brain was in overdrive. There was no way he could leave them here. Not now he'd seen it. Not now he'd smelled it.

This was about work. He was prioritising the needs of the labour suite above all others. That was what he was telling himself right now, but that was the only way he could make sense of the possibility that had just flown into his head.

'You have to get her out of here. A child with asthma can't possibly stay in an environment like this.'

This time she was blinking back tears. 'What choice do I have?' She sounded exasperated, her hand curled protectively around her daughter.

'You can stay with me.' The words were out before he even had a chance to think properly.

It made no sense. It made no sense whatsoever. He was a bachelor. After the last fourteen months he liked his solitude. His home was his salvation.

'What?' Bonnie straightened up. 'What do you mean?'

'I mean, you and your daughter can stay with me—

until you find something more suitable, of course. I have space in my house. You can stay with me.'

'No. No, we can't do that.' She was shaking her head. 'We don't even really know you.'

A wave of embarrassment came over him. After his behaviour this morning it was understandable that she was wary.

He took a deep breath. 'Look, Bonnie, I'm sorry about this morning. I know I came across as difficult.' He shook his head. 'But that's just me. It probably wasn't the ideal first meeting.' He held out his hands. 'But there's absolutely no way I'm letting you spend the next few days here with your daughter. Not while her health is at risk.'

It took a few seconds for the initial shocked expression on her face to disappear. Her tense shoulders gradually relaxed and she nodded slowly. Relief. That was what she was feeling now. It was palpable in the air all around them. The frown had disappeared from her brow and her blue eyes were focused clearly on him.

'You really mean it?' She seemed really hesitant.

It was clear she couldn't believe it. 'Freya and I can stay with you for a few days?' She glanced around her. 'We don't need to stay in this mouldy motel room?'

'Just until you find somewhere suitable.' From the expression on her face any minute now she would jump for joy.

'Of course.' Parts of his insides were doing strange twisting things. Making him think the word *no* but not letting it come out. This was work. They'd found a new temporary ward sister who needed a short-term solution for accommodation. It was logical. That was all.

'That's such a weight off my mind. Thank you, Jacob. Will your wife or partner be okay with this? The last thing I want to do is foist myself and a five-year-old on someone unexpectedly.'

Jacob gave the tiniest shake of his head. 'No wife. No partner.' He shrugged his shoulders. 'No time.' He squirmed a little saying those words out loud. Most single guys would probably be delighted to declare their freedom to the world. But for some reason it made him sound so isolated.

'And it won't be too much of an inconvenience to you?' Her voice rose a little at the end of the sentence, as if she were worried at any minute he might change his mind.

'How much trouble can a five-year-old be?' He was giving her a half smile as a whole surge of wariness swept over him. He had absolutely *no* experience with five-year-olds. He didn't even know how to have a conversation with one. He tried to rationalise things out loud. 'It makes sense. We need a ward sister to get on top of things in the labour ward. The last thing you need is for your daughter to be sick and to spend your time at work worrying about where you're staying. It's logical.'

She held out her hands. 'You'll need to give us a few minutes to pack. Thankfully we didn't really have a chance to unpack last night.'

It was almost as if Bonnie went into automatic pilot. She started pushing things haphazardly into a large blue case, then sat on it to close it. Now he'd made the offer it was clear she couldn't wait to get out of here—no matter how temporary the solution. And the truth was, he couldn't wait to get out of here either.

'Here,' he said, gesturing her to move. 'Let me. I'll push down and you can snap it shut.'

It did only take her a few minutes. But by the time she was finished there were four bulging suitcases for the car as well as the car seat. He gave her a wink. 'Just as well I brought my four-by-four and not my sports car. How on earth did you get down from the train with these?'

Something juddered through him. *Had he just winked at her?* What on earth was wrong with him? Since when did he do things like that?

This woman was having a strange effect on him.

But Bonnie didn't seem to notice. She just looked a little sheepish. 'It's a bit hard trying to ram all your worldly goods into some suitcases. Particularly when your five-year-old wants to bring all twenty of her favourite cuddly toys.' She sighed. 'I've got some stuff in storage as well at my mum and dad's. Once we find somewhere to stay I'll send for it.'

He picked up the first two cases and carried them out to the car. All of a sudden he felt as if he'd put his foot in his mouth. He wasn't trying to offend her. He'd spent the last year so focused on his treatment and keeping the department running that he hadn't bothered much with social niceties. Maybe it was time to start paying attention again.

Bonnie went to pay her bill as he loaded the last two cases into the car. 'You shouldn't have paid anything. That place is a disgrace.'

She strapped Freya back in and climbed into the passenger seat. 'Don't. He wanted me to pay for the whole week because we've left early.'

'I hope you refused.'

She gave him a wink. 'Of course I did.'

He started the car with a smile. Just as well he hadn't been driving. He'd have probably swerved off the road. She had seen the wink and had taken it as intended— in good humour. Thank goodness. He couldn't afford to tiptoe around someone who would be staying in his house. He must have been crazy inviting her to stay. *She* must have been crazy to accept. Either that, or she was desperate.

And he already knew that she was.

He had to keep remembering that. Otherwise his mind might start to drift in other directions. He'd never shared his house with a woman before. Let alone a woman and child. He was used to his own space. This had disaster written all over it.

His stomach started to churn a little. This was the craziest thing he'd ever done. He knew that his house was tidy—Monday was the day his housekeeper came. He'd texted her earlier and asked her to pick up some food for him. His fridge was currently bare. It was hardly hospitable to invite a mother and child back with not even a drop of milk in the fridge.

There. That was better. A mother and child seemed a much safer thought than anything that involved the name Bonnie.

He pulled up outside his Victorian town house. It had just started to rain and Bonnie pressed her nose up against the glass. 'Please tell me you only own part of that.'

He opened the car door. 'Nope. It's all mine. Including the ancient kennel in the back garden.'

He felt a little surge of pride in his heart that she liked his house. It was very traditional for Cambridge. Set in a residential area, in the middle of the city, the three-storey town house was just moments away from the river and college boathouses.

'You have a dog?'

Freya. He'd almost forgotten she was there. She had that expression on her face again. The little frown line across her forehead. She was standing in the rain staring up at the bay window at the front of the house. He pulled her hood up over her head. 'No. Sorry, I don't. I just have a really old kennel.'

He popped the boot and lifted out the first two cases, then walked up the path and deposited them at the doorway while he fished for his keys. 'Give me a sec,' he said as he opened the door and turned off the alarm. 'Go inside. I'll get the other cases.'

The rain was getting heavier now and it only took a few seconds to wrestle the other cases from the back of the car and get inside. He closed the door behind him and breathed a sigh of relief.

Home was usually his sanctuary. The place he came back to after work or treatment, closed the blinds and ignored the world. Chances were, he wouldn't get to do that any time soon. Thank goodness his treatment was over. Now he just had to wait for his results.

Bonnie had picked Freya up and carried her through the long corridor and turned left into the main lounge. He heard the little suck in of breath. What did that mean?

He dumped the cases at the door and followed her into the lounge. She spun around to face him. 'Wow. This place is just yours? It's gorgeous.' She set Freya down on the floor and walked over to the fireplace. 'This is just amazing. Does it work? Do you have a real fire on a winter's night?' She crouched down and touched the tile work around the fireplace.

He'd always been proud of his home, but for the first time he felt a little regretful. He touched the marble surround. 'No. I've never had the chimney swept. It is apparently in working order. I just never got around to it.' He pointed to the walls. 'I do have the original cast-iron radiators. So don't worry. You won't be cold.'

She shook her head. 'Oh, I'm not worried about being

cold.' She looked down. 'The floorboards are gorgeous too. Are they original?' She knelt down and ran her hand along the floor. He was learning quickly that Bonnie was a very tactile person.

'I sanded them down. It took about a year to do the whole house.'

She nodded in approval. 'I noticed the gorgeous geometric floor tiles on the way in too. I always wanted a hallway with those.' She looked a little lost in her own thoughts, then gave a little shrug. 'I'd be happy just to have a hallway right now.'

'Those tiles were hidden under the ugliest shag-pile carpet you've ever seen.'

She gasped. 'Really?' Then shuddered. 'What a crime to cover those up.'

'It probably saved them from being ruined. I've had them all coated now with something that should mean they last the next hundred years.'

She took a look around her. 'I'll never be able to afford a place like this. You're so lucky.'

Lucky. Now there was a word he'd never use to describe himself. Over the course of such an eventful day he'd realised how easy it was to be around Bonnie. Now it struck him how little she actually knew him. How little most of the staff at CRMU actually knew him. He could count on one hand the people he'd actually trusted with his secret. They knew how much he'd struggled this last year. How frustrated he'd been when he couldn't deal with patients because of the type of chemotherapy he was undergoing. How much he wanted just to get back to normal and do his job the way he always had.

Lucky. Maybe he was lucky. His cancer was treatable. Other types weren't. He'd managed to undergo his treatment quietly with only one day off work sick. Good planning had played a huge part in that. Having a cancer treatment team who were willing to allow him to start chemotherapy on a Thursday evening, which meant the after-effects didn't really hit until the Friday night, meant he could still work, then spend most weekends in bed to allow himself to recover.

But he still didn't feel lucky. His mother certainly hadn't been. She'd had the same type of cancer that he had—non-Hodgkin's lymphoma. It was generally thought that it wasn't an inherited disease. But tell that to the families where more than one person had it. There was just so much still to learn about these diseases. So many genes in the body where they still couldn't determine their purpose.

But his last treatment was finished now. In a few weeks' time he'd have his bloods rechecked to see if the treatment had worked and his cancer was finally gone. The whole black cloud that had been hanging over his head for the last fourteen months would finally be gone. Maybe. Hopefully.

Bonnie was still walking around. She had a little look of wonder on her face. As if she really did love the place. She stood with her back to the bay window and looked across the room. A smile lit up her face. She was obviously seeing something that he didn't.

'This place must be so gorgeous at Christmastime. I can just imagine it.' She spun around and held out her hands. 'A huge tree at this window that everyone out on the street can see.' She walked towards the fireplace again. 'One of those green and red garlands for the mantel, with some twinkling lights.' She turned back to the window. 'And some old-fashioned heavy-duty velvet curtains around the window.' She touched the white blinds that were currently in place and gave a little frown. 'Do you change these at Christmas? It's such a gorgeous bay window. You should make the most of it.'

He could almost hear the shutters clanging into place in his brain. He saw it. The pictures in her head that would never be in his. Never. He didn't do Christmas— hadn't since he was a young boy.

She couldn't possibly know. She couldn't possibly understand. He and his father had literally watched the life being sucked out of his mother. She'd died around Christmastime and the season celebrations had been a permanent reminder ever since. He hated Christmas. He'd always offered to work it, and since most of his colleagues had children they'd always been happy to accept his offer. He'd never hung a single decoration in his home. He didn't even own any.

He could see her gaze narrow ever so slightly as she looked more critically now around the whitewashed room with white window blinds. Apart from the wooden floor, the only thing that gave the room some colour was the dark leather suite.

He'd always loved his house. It suited his needs fine. He didn't want to accommodate anyone else's opinions or tastes.

He walked back out to the hall. Away from the look of expectation on Bonnie's face. Away from her smiling, overactive imagination. 'I don't really have time for Christmas, or to decorate. There's not much point. I'm always on duty at the hospital anyway. Come on, I'll show you both where your rooms are.'

He didn't even wait to see if she was following him. Just picked up the first two cases and headed to the stairs. Bonnie still had that glazed expression on her face. She touched the banister. 'This must be beautiful with tinsel wound around it.'

He swept past her on the staircase. 'Not going to happen. Not in this house.' He was done being subtle. She hadn't picked up on the first clues. He was going to have to hang a sign saying 'No Christmas' above the mantelpiece. What did it matter anyway—by Christmas she wouldn't be here. Not in his house anyway.

He paused at the landing, ignoring her puzzled expression and cutting her off before she had the chance to speak. 'There's three bedrooms on this floor—one of which is mine—and two bedrooms and a bathroom on the floor above. I think you and Bonnie might be better up there. More privacy for you both.'

More privacy for me too. He didn't want to wander along the hall half dressed to find a little red-haired girl with her disapproving glare.

He started up the other flight of stairs before Bonnie really had a chance to reply. The housekeeper had definitely been in today. The doors of both rooms were open and he could smell the freshly laundered linen on the beds. He put the cases in the first room that had a double bed. 'I'm assuming you'll sleep in here and Freya next door. There's a single in there. Bathroom's at the end of the hall.' He walked along the corridor and flicked the light switch in the white-tiled bathroom. He hadn't really thought about it before. Just about everything in this house was white.

He watched as Freya walked suspiciously into the single room, her eyes flitting from side to side. She looked at the single bed covered in a white duvet, the chest of drawers, and then turned around and walked back to Bonnie, wrapping her arms around her waist and cuddling her tight.

Her actions gave Jacob a start. There was nothing wrong with this room. It was fine. Why didn't she like it? He took a few seconds and looked again. Maybe the room was a little stark. Maybe it wasn't exactly welcoming for a little girl. But how on earth would he know what a little girl would like? It wasn't as if he'd had any practice. The kids he was generally around were only a few days or hours old.

'Maybe you'd like to sleep in with your mum?' He had no idea where that had come from. Chances were, he'd just committed some huge parenting faux pas. He was just struggling to understand Freya's reaction to the perfectly acceptable room.

Bonnie looked up and shot him a grateful glance. 'We'll play it by ear. Thank you, Jacob.'

He gave a relieved nod. 'Sorry, I didn't show you the kitchen or the back sitting room. It has a more comfortable sofa—and another TV and DVD player.' A thought darted into his brain. 'The only place I'd prefer Freya stay out of is my office downstairs.' The place was full of research about non-Hodgkin's lymphoma. Statistics for everything, including the most successful forms of treatment. Freya wouldn't be able to read any of that but Bonnie would if she followed Freya in.

'Absolutely no problem.' Bonnie had wound her hand through Freya's hair and was stroking the back of her neck. Did she know she was doing it? Or was it just a subconscious act?

'There's some food in the kitchen. Help yourself to anything that's in the fridge, freezer or cupboards.' He glanced at Freya. 'I'm not quite sure what Freya will like but my housekeeper picked up some groceries for me today. Or you could have some toast if you prefer?'

He had absolutely no idea what he was doing. This had been his craziest idea yet. A woman who was practically a stranger and a child who was clearly uncomfortable around him—and he'd invited them to stay in his home.

For the first time in a long time, Jacob Layton felt well and truly out of his depth.

Jacob was waiting for an answer. He had that anxious look on his face again. The one that kept appearing every few minutes. It was clear he wasn't used to having people in his house and she realised just what an inconvenience this must be to him. Her stomach flip-flopped with guilt. He must have regretted his offer as soon as the words had left his mouth.

But he seemed so anxious to please. It was almost cute. And she could bet that Jacob Layton had never been described as cute before.

She swallowed. She'd kill for a cup of tea right now. But it just didn't seem right to walk into someone else's kitchen and make yourself at home. 'I didn't mean to put you to so much trouble, Jacob. Please apologise to your housekeeper for me. I didn't mean to give her additional work.'

He waved his hand. 'You haven't. She shops for me on occasion anyway. I'm just not sure how much she'll have got as I didn't know I'd have guests. Check the fridge. I'll go and get your other cases.' He disappeared down the stairs as she stared at the bulging cases in the white room. Her blue case looked ready to explode. It was so out of place in here. A huge splash of colour against the stark white room. Thank goodness for the wooden floorboards. They added a little warmth about the place.

She shuffled over to the case, Freya still attached to her waist. It was clear her little girl was feeling overwhelmed by the whole situation. And to be truthful—she was too.

He had no idea what he'd let himself in for. Once she opened those cases his beautiful, pristine house would never look the same again. It wasn't that she was messy—she would never be messy staying as a guest in someone's house. It was just—once she opened the cases—things would start to get everywhere, as if they had self-migrating powers. And she wasn't quite sure how Jacob would feel about that. She let out a sigh and sat down on the bed, pulling Freya along with her. The comfortable mattress almost swallowed them up.

This place was a thousand times better than the motel. Here, she wouldn't be worried about Freya's asthma flaring up. The house was warm without being too hot. It was clean. It was spacious. They had their own rooms—they almost had their own floor.

Money. The thought came out of nowhere and she sat bolt upright. She hadn't offered him any money. There was no way she could stay here rent-free. It was quite obvious that Jacob was putting himself out for them. She would have to find a way to bring it up. But she had a bad feeling about how it would go.

Jacob. It was strange being in his house. *His home.* But that was just it. It didn't really feel like a home.

The white everywhere made it seem almost clinical. She would have imagined him staying in some brand-new luxury penthouse flat—not an old Victorian town house. It was beautiful. There was no doubt about that, and she hadn't even seen the kitchen yet.

But there were no pictures. No family photos. He hadn't even mentioned his family yet. There was no little sign of 'him' anywhere in the house. Who was Jacob Layton?

She ran her fingers across the bedspread. That was

what was wrong. This was a beautiful house. But it didn't feel like home. Why?

A house like this should exude warmth, character. And Jacob's house wasn't like that. She had the overwhelming urge to change the curtains in the lounge, to buy some different bedspreads for the white rooms and to add some accessories—some red towels in the white bathrooms, some pictures along the walls in the hall. A splash of colour was just what this place needed. She shook her head. This wasn't her home and she should just be grateful to have somewhere to stay. It was none of her business how Jacob chose to decorate his beautiful home.

'Come on, pumpkin. Let's leave the cases for now and go and find some dinner.' She took Freya's warm hand in hers and led her downstairs, blinking as she entered the kitchen. Just as she expected. White and chrome, all gleaming and sparkling.

But there was one nice little touch. The worktop wasn't granite like most designer kitchens. The worktop was a thick wooden polished surface that led to a deep white Belfast sink. It offset the rest of the white and chrome, giving the kitchen a little more warmth.

There was no kitchen table, just a central island with high black bar-style stools. She positioned Freya carefully on one and looked in the freezer. No—not a single thing.

She frowned and opened the fridge. Two steaks. One steak pie, some bacon, some eggs and two carefully wrapped bundles from the fishmongers. One labelled as cod in breadcrumbs. Even the fish fingers were posh round here.

Jacob appeared at her back as she was hunting for some oven trays and baking foil. 'Are you getting on okay?'

She nodded and smiled. 'We decided to eat first and

unpack later. We both had first days today and we're pretty wiped out.'

He opened a cupboard and took out some wine glasses, then glanced at Freya and swapped one for a tumbler. 'Would you like some wine?'

She shook her head. 'Honestly? I'm just too tired. I'd love a cup of tea though. And I still need to empty our cases. Could you show me where the washing machine is? I'd appreciate it if we could do some laundry.'

He stood up and opened a few cupboards. 'My house-keeper always buys some fruit and some biscuits— they're in here. Tea and coffee is here. If you turn the red button down on the tap you'll get boiling water.'

'From the tap?'

He nodded. 'Saves boiling the kettle—' he glanced sideways '—and it's too high up for Freya to reach. There's a proper cappuccino maker next to the oven if you prefer.' He gave a little smile. 'To be honest there's too many buttons. I've never used it. But the instructions are there—you're welcome to christen it if you wish.'

He pointed behind her as he ducked into a cupboard and pulled out a bottle of diet cola. 'Utility room is through there. There's a washing machine, tumble dryer and dishwasher, as well as another toilet and the door to the back garden. Freya's welcome to play out there if it's warm enough.' He gave a little grimace. 'I think the only thing you'll find out there is an old football.'

'Don't you have a dog kennel?'

They both turned to the unexpected little voice. Freya had been silent since she'd come downstairs. Jacob moved over next to her. 'I told you that in the car, didn't I? There is an old kennel out there. It must have belonged to the people who owned the house before I did. It still has the dog's name above the kennel.'

'What was his name?'

'How did you know it was a boy?' he answered quickly.

She shrugged. 'I guessed.' Bonnie was amazed. Freya had seemed a little overwhelmed earlier. But maybe she was starting to feel a little more comfortable in the house. She was glad that Jacob was making an effort with her daughter. She already felt as if they'd have to tiptoe round about him. Maybe it wouldn't be quite as awkward as she'd thought.

'Well, you were right. It was a boy. His name was Bones.'

Freya wrinkled her nose. 'Bones? That's a rubbish name for a dog.'

Bonnie couldn't help but laugh at her blunt response. Jacob leaned his elbow on the island. 'Really? That's what I thought too. What would you call a dog?'

Freya thought for a few seconds. 'Sandy. I'd like a little dog. One that's white and sandy coloured.' She leaned forwards and whispered conspiratorially. 'That's why I'd call him Sandy.'

Bonnie tapped Jacob on the shoulder as she poured the diet cola into Freya's tumbler. Not the ideal drink for a five-year-old—but she was just thankful that Jacob had anything at all that was suitable. She set about making a cup of tea for herself. 'Don't give her any ideas. One day it's a bichon frise, the next it's a terrier, the next a Havanese. Let's remember that most places we'll be renting won't accept pets. I keep trying to tell her that.'

He smiled conspiratorially at Freya and pretend whispered to her. 'I think you need to tell Mummy to find a house that takes dogs.' She almost fell over. She hadn't thought he had it in him. Jacob was full of surprises.

He walked over to the fridge and pulled out a silver

tray. 'Do you want to have fish too? My housekeeper seems to have bought plenty. She seems to have decided to feed me up. It will only take fifteen minutes.' He slid the sea bass into the oven next to Freya's fish fingers, then grabbed an oven tray, covered it in silver foil and tipped something from a plastic tub into it. He gave a shrug, 'Mediterranean crushed potatoes. I'm rubbish at shopping and cooking. My housekeeper always makes a few back-up meals for me. She says it's the only time my kitchen is put to good use.'

She gave an awkward nod and sat up on one of the stools, warming her hands on her teacup. This was all a little strange.

Jacob looked at her as he poured himself some wine. 'You okay?'

She sighed. 'It's been a big day. This morning I dropped my daughter at a brand-new school, took a bus ride through an unfamiliar city, was late for my first day at work. Accepted a temporary promotion, helped at the scene of an accident and moved into my boss's home. All in one day.'

He sipped his wine. 'I think I've got this one covered for you.'

'What do you mean?' She was curious.

He gave a little smile. 'One of my good friends is Scottish. I think this could be the "I'm completely knackered" answer.'

She burst out laughing and Freya's mouth hung open. 'What a terrible accent!' She lifted her cup of tea towards him. 'But the word is perfect, and, yes, it is the one I would have chosen. I'm completely and utterly knackered. I can't wait to climb into bed with Freya and go to sleep. I can guarantee you—we won't wake up until the alarm goes off.'

Something flickered across his face. 'I'm just glad that Freya will sleep safely. You must have had night-mares last night.'

She hesitated and gave a grateful nod. 'Jacob, we can't stay here without giving you some money. Can I give you what we would have paid for the motel?'

'No.' His answer came out a bit sharply and she started.

'It only seems fair,' she said slowly. 'I know we're imposing and you've already gone to too much trouble for us.' She gestured towards the oven. 'The food that you bought. I'll feel really uncomfortable if you don't let me contribute.'

He took a sip of his wine. 'Then feel really uncom-fortable—because I won't. It's only temporary. You'll find somewhere to stay soon. It's only a stopgap to give you some breathing space. We both know that. And any-way—you'll buy your own food for yourself and Freya. I just thought you wouldn't have had much opportunity be-tween arriving last night and coming to work today.' He gave a shrug of his shoulders. 'I don't want the new sister of the labour suite passing out from hunger tomorrow.'

He was so matter-of-fact about it. He made it sound so reasonable. Even though she knew it really wasn't.

She held up her cup of tea towards his. 'Thank you. But you need to know—I won't let this go. I'll keep hounding you.'

He clinked his glass against her cup. 'I'll look for-ward to it.'

His eyes connected with Bonnie's. That was the differ-ence between herself and her daughter. Bonnie's eyes were deep blue—almost hypnotising. Freya's were the more traditional pale blue.

From the second he'd offered her a place to stay he'd wanted to drag the words back. His stomach had churned and he'd conjured up a million different excuses to try to back out. But his integrity wouldn't let him—that, and the relieved expression on Bonnie's face when he'd made the offer. His guts had twisted at the thought of people in his home. His private place. But it wasn't quite as bad as he'd imagined. It was odd. The last person he'd shared a house with had been his father. It was amazing how long two people could live together while barely talking. Particularly when he'd told his father he wasn't the following the military family tradition and was going into medicine instead. His father had barely looked him in the eye after that.

Before dinner he led them through the rest of the house, showing them a dining room, the door to his study, the downstairs cloakroom and the back sitting room and conservatory.

'This house is just amazing, Jacob, and it's so close to the city centre. What do they call this street—millionaire row?' She was joking but he could see the weariness in her eyes. She'd been uprooted from a familiar home and ended up in a bad motel. Now she was going to be spending the next few weeks scouring around for houses to rent or buy, trying to work out if it was in an area she'd want her and Freya to stay in. All in the run-up to Christmas. Her brain must be currently whirring.

He laughed. 'No. Not quite. I bought it around ten years ago before the prices went crazy. It needed a lot of fixing up and I've just done a little bit at a time.'

'Well, I think you've done a good job. I hope I'll get a chance to have a walk around the area in the next few days. It would be good to get a bit more familiar with Cambridge.'

'If I get a chance, I'll show you and Freya around. Point out the places to visit and the places to avoid.' Where had that come from? It was so unlike him. He'd spent the last year living his life in a bubble. Hardly any interaction with friends and colleagues. The few people that he'd confided in about his condition had all offered to help in any way that they could. But offers of help made him feel vulnerable, at risk even.

Jacob had got through this life shutting off his feelings from the world. He hadn't even properly mourned the death of his mother. That wasn't the Layton way. Or so his father had told him. He'd very much instilled the stiff-upper-lip mentality into his son.

And even after all these years it was still there. It was partly the reason he'd never had a lasting relationship. He'd shuttered himself away for so long it felt normal now. And after a while his friends had stopped offering any assistance. Eventually even good friends got tired of being rebuffed.

Bonnie gave him a smile. 'Thanks, Jacob. That's really nice of you to offer.'

The timer on the oven sounded and Bonnie helped him to put the food onto plates. Instead of moving to the dining room, they stayed at the more informal island in the kitchen. By now, Freya was desperate to see the old kennel outside and invented an imaginary dog for her stay. But it was already dark and after she'd finished her fish fingers her little head started to nod.

Bonnie wrapped her arm around Freya's shoulders. 'I think it's time to get a little girl into her bath and into bed. To be honest, I could do with an early night myself. Once I've helped you clear up I think we'll both go to bed.' She stood up and gave him a wink. 'I don't want to be late for work tomorrow.' She gave a fake roll of her eyes. 'You've no idea what the boss is like.'

He let out a laugh and lifted the plates. 'Don't worry. I've heard about him. Forget about clearing up. I'll dump the dishes in the dishwasher and we're done.'

'You're sure?' She'd already picked up Freya and the little girl had snuggled into her shoulder.

'I'm sure. Goodnight, Bonnie. Goodnight, Freya.' It was odd—for the first time in a long time, Jacob actually felt at peace.

Then Bonnie spoiled it. She fixed on him with her unblinking blue eyes. 'Goodnight, Jacob, and thank you,' then turned and walked up the stairs.

There was nothing surer. The sight of Bonnie's backside in those jeans would stay with him well into the early hours of the morning.

CHAPTER FOUR

THERE WAS NO denying it. The labour suite had been in a complete muddle. Her mother would have called it a right guddle—a good Scots word. And she would have been right.

It seemed that in the few weeks since the sister had left, a new ordering system had come into place, and a new electronic system for recording staff working hours. No one on the labour suite had the time or motivation to learn how to use either and things were well behind.

Bonnie was lucky. There were other staff who offered to help. Isabel Delamere, an obstetrician on an exchange from Australia, was quick to give her the low-down on most members of staff. She wasn't a gossip. In fact, Bonnie got the impression that Isabel was quite the opposite. But she'd been new here herself and obviously wanted to help.

Hope Sanders, one of the other midwives, had been great. She'd quickly explained both new systems to Bonnie. It was strange. Bonnie had seen Hope talk to Jacob a few times. It was obvious they were friends. And the tall curly-haired blonde had already told her she was single. But Bonnie could tell there wasn't anything romantic between them.

If anything, Hope just seemed concerned about Jacob.

She was always reminding him about the number of hours he worked and telling him to get out a bit more.

Things were a little awkward on the ward. Both of them had decided it wouldn't be wise if the rest of the staff knew Bonnie and her daughter were staying with Jacob. It meant that she tried to jump out of the car before they reached the car park and other members of staff would notice them together. For the last few days things had been fine.

Well. That wasn't entirely true. She'd spent every night poring over the Internet looking at rental properties and houses for sale. Jacob had tried to be helpful. But Jacob's helpful had been telling her that one area where a house was for sale was less than salubrious and three of the rental properties had been similar. There was nothing else suitable in her price range. Trouble was, she'd moved here at the wrong time of year. Cambridge had lots of properties for rent, but most were rented by students and visiting lecturers for a year at a time. If she'd arrived a few months earlier there would probably have been lots of properties to view. Arriving in November? Not a chance.

Kerry, one of the midwives in the unit, leaned over the desk towards her. 'Bonnie, we've just had a call to say that Hayley Dickson is coming in, query spontaneous rupture of membranes. She's twenty-seven, and is thirty-six weeks pregnant with twins. We're expecting her in around an hour and I'll need some assistance. Any chance you can go for your lunch now?'

Bonnie smiled and nodded. 'My first twin delivery at Cambridge? Love to. Have you had lunch?'

Kerry nodded. 'It's only you that's still to go. Better hurry before there's nothing left in the canteen.'

Bonnie stood up. 'No problem. I'll be back in half an hour to help you get set up.'

She washed her hands and grabbed her bag. She was glad that the staff found her approachable and were happy to ask for assistance. It gave a bit of reassurance that they were accepting her as temporary sister around here.

The canteen was quiet. She grabbed a tuna sandwich and walked over to a table to join one of the other midwives that she'd met. Jessica Black worked in the special care baby unit. Her blond straight hair hung in a ponytail but her pretty face was marred by a frown as she stared out of the window.

'Mind if I join you?'

Jess started but gave a smile and waved at the empty seats across from her. 'By all means. Try and cheer me up if you can.'

Bonnie pulled out a chair. 'What's wrong? Man trouble?'

Jess rolled her eyes. 'As if. I wish. That would be easy to sort out.' She picked at her lunch. 'Family troubles. It's my parents' thirtieth wedding anniversary in a few weeks. It's been arranged for near Cambridge so I can't make an excuse not to go and I'm looking forward to it like a hole in the head.'

Bonnie was puzzled. 'Shouldn't that be something to celebrate?'

Jess sighed. 'It should. I love my parents. But it's yet another family event where I'll spend the whole time being compared to my sister. And will, yet again, be found lacking.'

'I can't believe that for a second. You've got a great job and career ahead of you. You're a gorgeous girl. What on earth does your sister have that you don't?'

Jess paused for a second and let out another big sigh. 'She's not just my sister. She's my twin. Abbie is perfect. She always has been. The sports star, top marks at school, the coolest boyfriend—you name it, Abbie's done it. I've spent most of my life living in her shadow. If Abbie preferred my Christmas presents to hers, she made such a scene she always got them. When I started midwifery training, she decided she wanted to do it too. Then, she decided she wanted the boyfriend I had.' She gave her head a shake. 'So, she got him. Along with the big white wedding and three perfect kids with another on the way.' She held out her hands. 'In fact, here is the only place where I'm known as anything other than "Abbie's sister".'

Bonnie was shocked by Jess's words. She reached over and squeezed her hand. 'Competitive siblings can be a nightmare. My ex-husband was like that with his brother. It made him even harder to live with.' She sucked in a breath. 'And if Cambridge Royal is like every other hospital I've worked in, you'll have heard that I found my ex-husband in bed with my best friend. So, I sympathise. At least I had the option of walking away. I don't need to look at them together.' She leaned back and took a sip of her coffee. 'It sucks that you have to do that.'

Jess burst out laughing and reached over towards Bonnie. 'Yes, the hospital grapevine is in full flow and I love that you just say it like it is.'

Bonnie shrugged. 'After thirty-two years there's not much point in changing the habit of a lifetime.'

Jess gave her a rueful stare. 'I might have heard that about you too. Men suck. Unfortunately, men are my biggest issue. Or namely the fact I don't have one. That's the reason I'm dreading the anniversary party so much. Everyone is just waiting for me to produce who is going to be Mr Jessica Black and create the two-point-four kids we're supposed to have.'

Bonnie took a bite of her tuna sandwich. 'Can't you take a friend?'

'Yeah, but the friend would need to reach my family's exacting standards. They would have to be devastatingly handsome, completely charming and totally unfazed by my sister trying to be the centre of attention.'

Bonnie gave a little smile. 'I have to say, there's more than a few handsome guys around here. Can't you ask one to accompany you?'

Jess frowned. 'Like who?'

Bonnie swallowed and tried to appear casual. 'What about Jacob Layton?'

Jess waved her hand. 'Oh, he's handsome enough but way too grumpy.'

Bonnie tried not to let the wave of relief sweeping over her be obvious. 'Aaron Cartwright, the infertility specialist? An American might go down well.'

She smiled and shook her head. 'He might. But he's not for me. He's too committed to his work. That's the problem with most of the guys around here.'

Bonnie thought again. She was just here. But she'd met most of the consultants in the last few days. 'I've got it. What about an Australian, then, Sean Anderson, the obstetrician that arrived just a few weeks before me?'

'Are you serious?' Jess laughed and wagged her finger. 'I'm going to forgive your observational skills, Nurse, because you've just started. But have you noticed how jumpy Isabel is since he got here?'

Bonnie racked her brains. Isabel was also an Australian obstetrician. Bonnie hadn't connected the two, but maybe there was something... She'd been warm and friendly towards Bonnie since she arrived. She shook her head and shrugged. 'I've never seen them together, so I can't say I've noticed.'

Jess raised her eyebrows. 'She's like a proverbial cat

on a hot tin roof. Mark my words, there's some history there. I'm not getting embroiled in that.'

Bonnie took a final bite of her tuna sandwich. When she'd finished chewing she had the perfect answer. 'I've got it. Why didn't I think of him before? You've got the perfect answer right under your nose. Dean Edwards, the SCBU doctor.'

Something flickered across Jess's eyes. Bonnie was on it in an instant.

'What? Has something happened between you two already?'

Jess almost choked. 'No. Absolutely not. But I'll be the only one. He has a different lady for every day of the week. His phone goes off *constantly*.'

Bonnie took a sip of her tea and sat back in her chair. 'Dean's a ladies' man? Who has he dated at work?'

Jess was quick to shake her head. 'Oh, no. He doesn't date anyone at work.' She held out her hands. 'But that leaves the rest of the world wide open for him.'

'And you struck off his list?' Drat. That came out too bluntly. She'd only met Jess on a few occasions.

But it was just the two of them and Jess looked up from her coffee, her light brown eyes rueful. Maybe it was easier to open up to someone who was new?

She blew out a long, slow breath from her lips. 'I guess so. He wouldn't look at me anyway—and even if he did, once he met Wonder Sister he'd be entranced by her. They all are. It wears pretty thin.'

Bonnie reached out towards her again. 'You're a gorgeous girl, Jess. It would be wrong of me to say anything about your sister, but, to be honest, she seems like a piece of work. You've got much more integrity than that, and somewhere—' she held up her hands '—out there, is a man who is just waiting to find a woman like you. You'll probably find him when you least expect to.' She glanced at the clock. 'I'm sorry but I better go. We've got a woman expecting twins due in.' She put her plate and cup on the tray and winked at Jess. 'I gave you the option of three gorgeous men and you said no to all of them. Don't let it be said that you're picky.'

Jess winked back and put her plate on her tray, standing up and walking towards the catering trolleys. 'You gave me the option of *four*, Bonnie. Now I'm wondering if you're keeping one to yourself.'

And she left, before Bonnie could pick her chin off the floor and stop kicking herself.

By the time she reached the ward she could feel herself blushing like crazy. This was ridiculous. No one knew she was staying at Jacob's. Everything at work was entirely professional.

Everything at home was entirely professional too. But Jacob was surprising her. For a guy that acted as though he would run a million miles from kids, he'd been surprisingly good with Freya. Yes, he was still a bit awkward, but he was definitely making an effort. And that mattered. A lot.

It was a dangerous line. If he hadn't been friendly, they could have felt like trespassers in his home. Jacob still didn't give much away. He was obviously a private person. And that was fine. Except five-year-olds weren't always good at knowing when to stop asking questions.

He met her at the doors of the ward. 'You're helping with the twin delivery?'

She grinned. 'I am. Is she your patient? Anything I should know?'

In a labour unit some women would be classed as midwifery care and some as medical care. Any woman with a multiple pregnancy automatically fell under medical care as they were at higher risk of complications. An average woman, with a normal pregnancy, could come into the unit and not come into contact with a medic at all. She would be delivered by the midwives and her follow-up care carried out by them. Babies were different—they were always checked over by a paediatrician.

Bonnie dumped her bag as Jacob kept pace with her. 'Hayley Dickson has had a textbook pregnancy but her blood pressure has gone up a little in the last two weeks. I'm actually glad she's gone into spontaneous labour because I was considering inducing her. She's been scanned for the last few weeks. No problems with the babies. It's non-identical twins and both babies are around six pounds.'

'Does she know what she's having?'

He shook his head. 'She didn't want to know.'

Bonnie smiled. 'Do you?'

'I might do—' he tapped his mouth '—but my lips are sealed. Let's go and introduce Mum to these beautiful babies.' He put his hand on Bonnie's shoulder. 'If it's okay with you, I'd like to let you and Kerry take the lead. I'm only here if there are any issues. I'll set up the epidural I know she wants. But Hayley is keen to have a normal delivery.'

Bonnie gave a nod. 'No problem. I'll go and pick up the cots, be back with you in a minute.'

She was glad that Jacob didn't want to try and take over and respected the birthing plan his patient had decided on. Sometimes medics could be a bit overzealous. She hated when that happened.

She collected the cots and baby warmers and headed back into the room. Kerry gave her a nod as she entered. 'Hayley, this is Bonnie, our new ward sister. She'll be helping with the delivery. Bonnie, this is Hayley and her husband, Jordan.'

Bonnie walked straight to the sink to wash her hands. 'Pleasure to meet you, Hayley. I'm really looking forward to meeting these two new babies.' She nodded towards the cots. 'As soon as the babies are out we'll have one of our paediatricians check them over. After you've had a cuddle, of course.'

Hayley gave a nervous smile, then grimaced as another contraction hit. 'I didn't expect these to be coming so quickly.'

Kerry had already completed all the paperwork and hooked Hayley up to the monitors. One was monitoring her babies, the other checking her blood pressure.

Jacob appeared at Bonnie's back, pushing a trolley with the equipment for the epidural. He gave a nod to Kerry. 'Have you done a check yet?'

Kerry nodded. 'Yes, we're good to go. Hayley is five centimetres dilated and the first baby is head down and in a good position.'

Jacob smiled. 'Perfect.' He sat next to Hayley to explain the procedure. It only took him a few minutes. 'Once the catheter is in place it will only take twenty minutes for the full effect. We'll keep an eye to make sure it doesn't slow your labour, but I suspect everything will be fine.' He gave Bonnie a little nod to help position Hayley on her side.

He was an expert. He had the catheter safely slid into place easily and the medication started. Bonnie stayed in the room with Kerry and they monitored Hayley's contractions.

Things went smoothly. Around two hours later the first little baby delivered easily. Bonnie quickly checked over the baby's mouth and breathing before setting the naked little baby on his mother's chest. 'You have a beautiful boy. Do you have a name yet?'

Hayley's husband couldn't wipe the dopey new-dad smile from his face. 'Dillon. We're going to call him Dillon.'

Sean came into the room with a smile. 'Perfect. I'm just in time. I'm Dr Anderson. I'll check your little man over in a few seconds, folks.'

He spoke with Jacob for a few minutes, checked Dillon over and declared him well with perfect APGARs. He gave them a little nod. 'I'll be back again when your next baby arrives. Good luck, guys.'

Kerry stayed with the new baby for another few minutes while Bonnie checked over Hayley again. The labour progressed quickly with the next baby's head being delivered; however, within a few seconds Bonnie frowned as another contraction hit. She turned rapidly to Jacob, keeping her voice very calm.

'I think we've got a shoulder dystocia.' Jacob moved over to the bed immediately but Bonnie had things under control. 'Hayley, your second baby has got a little stuck—their shoulder is stuck behind your pubic bone. Dr Layton and I are going to help you change position to try and get your baby out as soon as possible. I need you to stop pushing for a second until we help you into position.'

Jacob didn't interrupt at all. He just positioned himself at the side of the bed. Bonnie kept talking calmly and smoothly. 'We're going to do something called the McRoberts manoeuvre. I need you to lie on your back and pull up your legs as far as you can. Kerry will help on one side, and Dr Layton on the other. This will make it easier to get your baby out.' Kerry handed the little boy back over to his dad.

Bonnie gave a little nod to Jacob. 'Dr Layton is going

to push down on your tummy when you have the next contraction. This should free your baby's shoulder. It might be a little uncomfortable.' Bonnie glanced at the clock. She had to keep watch. A baby's umbilical cord could become compressed with shoulder dystocia. If they didn't get the baby out in the next few minutes, Hayley would need to go for an emergency Caesarean section.

The contraction hit right on cue. Bonnie eased her hands in to give a gentle pull on the baby as Jacob attempted to press the pelvic bone and release the baby's shoulder. After a few tense seconds, Hayley gave a yelp and the baby slid into Bonnie's hands.

Kerry had already sounded the alarm and Sean was waiting with outstretched arms to check over the baby. He only took a few minutes. It was important. Babies who had shoulder dystocia could have damage to the nerves in their shoulder, arm and hand. Some could have breathing difficulties if their cord had been compressed. But after a few minutes Sean pronounced the baby well. 'Congratulations, Mum and Dad, here's your new baby girl.'

Hayley and Jordan beamed. Bonnie stayed in position. After a few minutes Hayley delivered her placenta and Bonnie did her further checks. 'Have you got a name for your daughter?'

Hayley nodded. 'Carly. We're going to call her Carly.'

Kerry came over with the other baby. 'Dillon and Carly. They're beautiful names for your children. Congratulations.' She handed Dillon back over to his dad. 'Dillon was six pounds twelve, and Carly six pounds four. Good weights. Sean said he'd be back to check them again later but there's no reason for them to go to Special Care.'

Hayley and Jordan smiled at each other. They were

clearly in the new parenthood haze. Bonnie remembered it well.

Her heart sank a little—just as it always did at this stage. Robert, her ex, had never looked at her the way Jordan was looking at his wife. Robert had just looked permanently stunned. The same expression he'd had on his face when she'd found him in bed with her best friend. He hadn't been ready for marriage. With hindsight, they both hadn't.

Robert had been her boyfriend for barely a year when she'd fallen unexpectedly pregnant. His parents were traditionalists and had wanted them to get married. And now, Bonnie realised she'd been more swept away with the *idea* of being in love, rather than actually *being* in love. Maybe, at heart, she'd always known that Robert wasn't marriage material.

But what hurt most of all, despite her best efforts, was the fact he hadn't made any attempt at all to see Freya since they'd separated. It turned out Robert hadn't been father material either.

Cambridge was the chance of a new start. She didn't want to make the same mistakes again. She was determined not to get swept away in some ill-fated romance. Not when she had Freya to think about.

She loved her job. She always had. But sometimes, especially at an emotional delivery, she was struck by the connection between the parents of the new baby. Freya was everything to her. But sometimes it made her a tiny bit envious that she was missing out on something she'd never experienced.

It was pathetic really. Most people didn't get the fairy tale. Most people got relationships that were hard work—and she knew that. But it didn't stop her craving the impossible.

She tidied up in the room and got one of the domestics to make Hayley some tea and toast. Most women said that their post-delivery tea and toast was the best in the world.

Kerry tapped her on the shoulder. 'It's nearly your finishing time. I'm going to help Hayley with breast-feeding and will hand over to the next shift. Thanks for the help, Bonnie.'

Bonnie gave a smile. 'No problem, you're welcome.' She took the dirty laundry with her to the sluice, disposed of it and washed her hands again.

Jacob appeared at her back. 'I think that was one of the smoothest shoulder dystocia deliveries I've ever seen. Good call.'

Bonnie shook her head. 'That was pure luck. We both know things could have been different. I was actually breathing a sigh of relief as soon as that baby came out.'

Jacob rested his hand on the small of her back. 'Believe me, so was I. I didn't like the thought of a quick sprint down the corridor to Theatre.'

She could feel his warm hand through her thin scrubs. The warmth was radiating across the small of her back. When was the last time a man had touched her? She couldn't even remember.

She turned her shoulder just a little so she was looking up at him. She hadn't moved enough to let his hand fall. She didn't want it to break contact with her. 'Thank you, Jacob,' she said quietly.

'What for?' He tilted his head to the side. She was only inches away from those green eyes that sparkled with flecks of gold. This was the closest she'd ever been to him. She could see the tiny emerging shadow of stubble along his chin—even though she knew he'd shaved this morning. Her fingers itched to reach up and touch.

The weariness that had been on his face the first day

she'd met him had seemed to gradually disperse. On occasion, Jacob still looked tired. But there had been something else that first day—a little despair? Jacob was still a mystery to her. The only thing she knew for sure was that he didn't have a woman in his life and for some reason that made her happy. Not that she'd ever admit that to anyone—not even Jessica.

'For not interfering,' she was whispering, even though there was no need. The rush and bustle of the ward was still going on in the corridor outside, but this seemed like a private conversation. 'For not coming over all "doctor" and trying to take over. For giving me a chance to do my job.'

He leaned forwards just a little. One inch. That was the space currently between them. She held her breath. If she breathed out right now, her warm breath would touch his skin.

But there was a problem. As she'd breathed in, she'd breathed in *him*. Jacob. The faintest aroma of this morning's aftershave. The scent of his skin. She could almost swear she'd just breathed in a whole host of pheromones. What other explanation could there be for the fact she was feeling the slightest bit light-headed? She'd never been light-headed in her life.

'I'll always give you the space to do your job, Bonnie. From what I've seen you're excellent at it. I have faith you. The staff have faith in you. The patients have faith in you. You're a real asset to Cambridge Maternity. And I look after my staff.'

Her lungs were going to explode. She had to breathe out. She really did. Her insides were all over the place. It was the way he'd said it. The way he'd looked into her eyes and told her he had faith in her. She leaned back a little against his hand and tilted her chin up towards him. 'Thank you, Jacob.'

They froze. Neither of them moving. Their eyes locked together.

'Bonnie, can you just sign…? Oh, sorry.'

They sprang apart. It was stupid. They hadn't been doing anything but Bonnie could feel the colour rushing into her face.

Ellis, one of the midwives, was standing with a delivery note in her hand. Her eyes darted between them; it was quite obvious she was cringing and that made Bonnie do the same.

'That's fine, Ellis. I was just washing up after the twin delivery. Did you hear that things went well?' She was back into professional mode. She didn't even look back, just took long strides towards Ellis, taking the delivery note from her hand and walking over to the nurses' station, pulling a pen from her pocket.

She was trying to appear as calm and professional as possible. As if nothing at all had been going on between them. Because that was true. Nothing had been going on between them.

So why was her heart thudding against her chest and why did her cheeks feel as if they were on fire? And why was Ellis looking at her as if she would be the next topic of conversation on the hospital grapevine?

Ellis took the paperwork and disappeared back down the corridor. Bonnie sucked in a deep breath. What on earth was wrong with her? She'd almost wanted him to kiss her in the sluice at work. Even the thought of that sent a shiver down her spine—it was hardly the most romantic place in the world.

But it hadn't been about the place. It had been about the moment. The feel of Jacob's hand at the small of her back and the way she could see all the tiny lines around his perfect green eyes.

She squeezed her eyes shut. Even her thoughts were getting ridiculous. She had to speak to him. She had to try and understand what was going on. She had to draw a line here. She wasn't looking for any kind of romance. And definitely not with her new boss—no matter how much he just made her tingle. She spun around towards the sluice again.

But Jacob was gone.

CHAPTER FIVE

SOMETHING WAS DIFFERENT. Something had changed. And Jacob couldn't quite put his finger on what it was.

All he knew was he was currently sitting on his sofa watching an animated movie with a five-year-old. If someone had told him two weeks ago this was what he'd be doing he'd never have believed it.

'Who's your favourite dwarf?' whispered Freya. She'd insisted on the main light being turned off and eating ice cream as if they were at the movies. He'd never really developed a taste for ice cream but rocky road was hitting the spot.

'I like that one,' he said, pointing at the screen.

'He's my favourite too.' She jumped up and a big dollop of ice cream landed on his lap. 'Oops,' she said.

He shrugged and scooped the ice cream off his jeans with his fingers and dumped it in his mouth. Freya went into uncontrollable kinks of laughter.

All he knew for sure was that the big black cloud that felt as if it were permanently circling above his head had moved a little higher for the past two weeks. Maybe it was the fact that he was now in the waiting cycle. His treatment was over. He didn't feel quite so snappy. He certainly didn't feel so tired. And he was free to work with patients again the way he had before.

Something had definitely improved his mood. Even the junior doctors, who constantly got everything wrong and couldn't do the most basic of procedures, weren't annoying him as much as usual. He'd only thrown one out of Theatre the other day, instead of the usual four. People would think he was getting soft. He just wasn't quite sure if it was the treatment that had improved his mood or the home circumstances.

Living with Bonnie and Freya was certainly out of his normal experience. Freya had a way of winding him around her little finger. He wasn't quite sure if it was a five-year-old's mastermind plot, or if she did it purely unintentionally.

She jumped up from the sofa and over to her school bag, which was lying on the floor. 'Look at this!' she said as she pulled out a crumpled drawing. 'I made this for you at school today.' It was a painting of a man—with very big ears. He couldn't help it—he started to laugh.

She bounced back up on the sofa next to him. 'It's you. Do you like it?' Her little face was so expectant, just waiting for his approval.

He touched his ears. 'Are they really this big?'

'Yes,' she said without a moment's hesitation. 'Can we put it up on the fridge? That's where my mummy used to put my pictures.' She tugged at his hand and he let her pull him up and lead him through to the kitchen.

Bonnie was wiping a glass bowl clean as they walked through. 'Look what I made for Jacob,' Freya shouted as she waved the picture. 'We're going to put it up.'

Bonnie glanced at the picture and tried to stifle a laugh. 'I think that's lovely, honey,' she said. She raised her eyebrows at Jacob. 'Wait and I'll find you something to put that up with.' She opened a nearby drawer and pulled out a fridge magnet he didn't even know he owned. It seemed impolite not to put it up so he stuck it on the fridge.

Freya's little face was beaming. 'Come on,' she said, tugging at his arm again. 'My favourite song's about to start.'

He'd always loved his home. His sanctuary. His way of getting away from the outside world. But although his peace had been shattered, it was nowhere near as invasive as he might have thought.

He almost looked forward to coming home to them at night. And he couldn't work out why. Maybe it was the distraction. He didn't have time to think about the stuff hanging over his head. He didn't have time to consider what he would do if the test results weren't good—if the non-Hodgkin's lymphoma hadn't been halted in its tracks.

He didn't have time to remember how his mum had died of the horrible disease and how he could have the same future ahead of him. These were the things that used to spin around his head every night when he went to bed.

'Jacob, *come on*.' The little voice was impatient. He hadn't even realised that he'd been staring at Bonnie's backside in her snug jeans again. She spun around and gave a little smile as she put some cutlery back in a kitchen drawer.

She looked relaxed. She looked happy. She looked comfortable in his home. Something flipped over inside. He wasn't quite sure how he felt about all this.

She tilted her head to the side. 'Should I get us some wine to see us through the rest of the movie?' She was smiling again.

He gave a nod as he let Freya lead him back through to the front room and he heard the clink of glasses being pulled from the cupboard.

Their *almost* kiss in the sluice would no doubt haunt his dreams tonight.

What had happened?

He knew it was something. It was definitely something.

There had been a tiny moment when...just *something* could have happened. He'd felt it. And he was pretty sure she'd felt it too. He'd seen it in her all too expressive eyes.

They'd spent the last week tiptoeing around each other. But that hadn't stopped the buzz in the air between them. It hadn't stopped the way their gazes kept connecting with each other.

He'd spent so long concentrating on his disease and trying to get well again that he was out of practice with all this. But even though it was winter, the temperature here was definitely rising.

It was official. Bonnie Reid was keeping him awake at night.

But why did that seem like a good thing and not a bad?

It was her day off and she was prowling around the house. She couldn't help it. This weekend she would be working on Saturday as part of her rota for the hospital. It was fine. Lynn was happy to have Freya for the day and planned to take her and her boys to London Zoo.

But Bonnie wasn't used to having time to herself. She'd cleaned what she could without offending the housekeeper. She'd learned very quickly what was unacceptable for her to do in the house. All her and Freya's laundry was washed and ironed and sitting in neat piles. The beds were made, the shopping done.

She gave a little shudder. The house was getting cold. There had been a dip in the temperature in the last few days and she wasn't quite sure how the heating worked in this house. She wasn't quite sure how Jacob would feel if he found out she was tampering with the settings on his heating. She walked across the front room, her footsteps echoing on the wooden floorboards, her hand running across the top of the mantelpiece.

There was an ornamental coal scuttle at her feet. She knelt down. It was filled with real coal. Jacob had said he hadn't got round to having the chimney swept.

She gave another shudder. Nothing would be nicer at this time of year than a real fire burning in this gorgeous fireplace.

She stood upright. That was what she could do. Jacob didn't seem to have any objections to a real fire. He'd just made it sound as if he hadn't got round to it. He wouldn't accept any money from her and, to be honest, it felt a little embarrassing. Maybe paying to have the chimney professionally swept would be a way to try and repay him a little for his kindness?

She didn't hesitate. This was the best idea she'd had in a while. She walked out to the hallway and dug around for the phone book. They were in the middle of Cambridge. There were lots of traditionally built houses around here. There must a local chimney sweep.

Jacob was on call. He might even not be home at all tonight. Sometimes he ended up just staying at the hospital if he was on call. As the consultant he would be called if there was any emergency with a patient. He'd already told her that he wasn't entirely sure that all the junior members of staff would page him. Some of them still seemed a little nervous around him. She'd tried not to laugh when he'd said that to her.

She picked up the phone and dialled. By the time Jacob got home tonight—or maybe tomorrow morning—she'd have a lovely fire burning in the fireplace, heating up the whole house and giving the place a more homely feel.

He'd love it. She was sure he would.

The first thing he'd noticed was the strange smell. Ever since Bonnie had arrived his house had smelled of those clean laundry candles that she insisted on lighting everywhere. They actually made his nose itch but he wasn't inclined to tell her.

She'd waved some red and green ones under his nose the other night and told him she'd bought some Christmas spice candles. If this was what they smelled like he'd be blowing them straight out.

She still hadn't picked up on his hints about Christmas. The main fact being he just didn't do it.

There was a strange noise to his left. It sounded like a sniffle. Or more like a sob.

He sneezed. Something was definitely irritating him.

'Jacob? Is that you?'

Bonnie. Her voice sounded panicked. He dropped his bag at the door and lengthened his stride, walking into his front room.

Or walking into the room that used to be his front room.

Bonnie was on her hands and knees on the floor, a basin next to her, scrubbing away at the floorboards. Freya was sitting on a towel on the faraway leather sofa playing with her dolls.

He sucked in a breath at the sight of his perfect white walls.

They weren't perfect any more. There was a huge black streak that seemed to have puffed out from the fireplace and left an ugly, angry, giant-sized handprint on the wall.

Bonnie jumped up to speak to him. Soot was smudged across her cheeks and forehead, even discolouring her dark auburn hair. The front of her T-shirt was dirty, as were the knees of her trousers. 'Oh, Jacob. I'm so sorry. I thought I would have a chance to clean this up before you got home.'

He stepped forwards into the room and held out his hands. 'What on earth happened?'

Freya tutted from her sofa and shook her head. 'Naughty Mummy.' She fixed her eyes on Bonnie. 'Told you,' she said in the voice of someone at least fifty years older than her.

Tears streaked down Bonnie's face. 'I thought it might be a nice idea to get the chimney swept for you. You know—so you could come home to a nice warm fire. The house was so cold today. So I contacted a chimney sweep. And they seemed so professional. They even put a covering on the floor and some kind of plastic seal around the fireplace. But when he swept the chimney, there must have been a gap.' She turned to face the blighted wall again as her voice wobbled. 'And it just seemed to go everywhere. And they tried to clean up, they really did. And they've promised to come back tomorrow and re-paint the walls.'

He should be angry. But Bonnie was babbling. Just as she had that first day he'd met her. Just as she did when she was really, really nervous and thought she'd just blown things.

It was kind of endearing. But he'd never tell her that.

'Okay,' he said quietly.

She looked confused. Another tear streaked down her smudged face. 'Go and get washed up. I'll finish the clean-up.'

He was too tired to be angry. He'd wanted to come

home to a quiet house and rest. But the days of coming home to a quiet house were over. He could never imagine a house being quiet while Freya stayed there. She was questioning. She was curious. She was relentless.

Her head bobbed up from the menagerie of dolls she had accumulated on the other sofa. She shot him a smile. 'Hi, Jacob. How many babies did you see today?'

'Four,' he said promptly.

This had turned into a game. She asked every day. She frowned at him. 'Just four. Your record is six. You'll need to do better.'

'I agree.' He nodded towards Bonnie. 'On you go. Go and get showered. Freya will be fine.'

Bonnie still seemed surprised by his mediocre reaction. The truth was he was surprised by his reaction too. If he waited to see the chimney sweep tomorrow the reaction might not be quite so contained. But he wouldn't do that either.

He noticed the extra coal scuttle by the fire that contained wood-burning logs. Bonnie must have bought them to help light the fire.

When was the last time someone had done something like this for him? Sure, a few of his friends had offered help when they knew about his diagnosis. Hope and Isabel were the only two people—apart from his consultant—in the entire hospital who knew about his diagnosis. He'd worked with Hope for years and even though Isabel had only arrived a few months ago he'd known straight away she was completely trustworthy. When she'd caught him being sick in the sluice one day she'd just pulled the door closed and come over and asked what was wrong.

Both tried to help by feeding him various items of food. Hope had even tried to bake chocolate muffins for him and Isabel had handed him some tubs of beef casserole to stick in the freezer. Anything to get him to eat and keep his strength up. But he was embarrassed to say he'd only been minimally grateful. He was so focused on people not knowing what was wrong that he didn't really want to accept help.

This felt different. This was nothing about his illness. Bonnie knew nothing about that at all—and that was the way he liked it. The last thing he wanted to see on her face was pity.

This was something spontaneous. Something completely unique to him and her. Of course, she currently felt indebted to him. And that did kind of irk. But the fact she'd wanted to do something for *him*...just warmed him from the inside out.

He finished scrubbing the floor and carried the basin of dirty water back through to the kitchen, scrubbing his hands and turning the oven on for dinner. He put on the TV for Freya and headed upstairs into the shower. It only took two minutes to wash the smell of the hospital from his skin and hair, and pull on some jeans and a T-shirt.

As he headed back along the corridor Bonnie passed him on the stairs carrying Freya in her arms. 'Sorry,' she whispered. 'I made her dinner earlier and she's knackered. I'm just going to put her to bed. I didn't get a chance to put anything on for our dinner.'

Jacob noticed the circles under her eyes. He didn't want her to feel as if she had to do anything for him. 'How about I make it simple? Beans on toast?'

She smiled. It was the first genuine smile that he'd seen today. 'Perfect. Thank you.'

His culinary skills were just about up to beans on toast. He opened a bottle of white wine and spent a few minutes setting a new fire and lighting it. As his fingers touched the coal he was swamped by a whole host of memories. Last time he'd lit a fire he'd been trying to keep his shivering mother warm. She'd been at the stage when she'd been permanently cold, even though their house hadn't been cold.

Once she'd died, he'd never gone to the bother of cleaning out the fireplace and restocking it. Neither had his father.

The fire lit quickly. Probably due to the modern fire-lighters. By the time he'd finished the dinner in the kitchen and walked back through with them both on a tray, Bonnie was sitting on the leather sofa, mesmerised by the fire. She jumped when he set the tray down on the low wooden table. 'Give me a sec,' he said, before returning with the wine and two glasses.

Her freshly washed dark auburn hair was piled up in a loose knot on top of her head, with a few little curl-ing strands escaping. She'd changed into her favourite jeans and a gold T-shirt with a few scattered sequins that caught the flickering flames from the fire. Her pale skin glowed in the light.

She sighed as he poured the wine and she settled the plate on her knees. 'I don't know if I deserve this.'

Jacob looked at her sideways. He couldn't hide the smile on his face. She seemed so despondent. 'I'm not sure you do either. But it's either we drink wine together, or we fight. Take your pick.' He held up his glass to-wards her.

She paused for a second before catching a glimpse of the laughter in his eyes, then lifted her glass and clinked it against his. 'I'm too tired to fight. I'll just drink the wine.'

They ate companionably together. Finishing the first glass of wine, then pouring another. Jacob hadn't bothered to put the TV or radio on. The only noise was the hiss and cracks coming from the fire.

Bonnie pulled her feet up onto the sofa, giving him a glimpse of her pink-painted toes.

'It's amazing, isn't it?'

He nodded. Watching the fire was quite mesmerising. He could easily lose a few hours a night doing this, particularly if he had a warm body lying next to him on the sofa. His guts twisted. Why hadn't he done this before?

'I'm sorry about the wall,' she whispered again.

His eyes fixed on hers in the flickering firelight. They gleamed in the orange and yellow light. He looked over to the black ugly mark on the wall and couldn't help but start to laugh.

It was hideous. But it could be fixed. By tomorrow it would be freshly painted and forgotten about. His shoulders started to shake, the wine in his glass swaying from side to side.

'What did you say when it happened?' He could barely get the words out for laughter.

She started to laugh too and shook her head. 'You've no idea. I was in the kitchen with Freya and I just heard this whooshing noise and a thump. The guy landed on his backside in the middle of the floor. He looked as if he was about to be sick.'

Now the laughter had finally started she seemed relieved to get it out. 'Then I came through and just burst into tears. I don't think that helped him.'

'I'll bet it didn't.'

He turned towards her on the sofa, his arm already stretched behind her head. It was only natural she turned towards him too.

'Please tell me you're not really mad with me.'

He shook his head and reached his finger up to touch

her cheek. He didn't even think before he did it. It just seemed like the most natural act in the world. The act he'd wanted to do a few days before in the sluice room.

'I'm not mad at you. What you did was nice. It was thoughtful.' He gave a little shrug. 'I always meant to get around to it. It just never happened.' His voice tailed off a little. 'Other stuff got in the way.'

Her hand came up and rested on his bare arm. 'What other stuff?'

It was like a whole host of tiny electric shocks racing up his arm. He could feel the warmth of her skin next to his. All he wanted to do was grab her whole body and press it against his. Skin against skin.

'Nothing important. Work, that kind of stuff.' He didn't want to go there. Not with Bonnie. He didn't want to have any of those kinds of conversations with Bonnie. This thing between them. He didn't know what it was. But it seemed almost unreal. Not really acknowledged. Not really known by anyone but them.

She hesitated but didn't move her hand. She left it there in contact with his skin.

'I need some advice. I saw some other possible rentals today and one small flat that I could afford to buy. You need to tell me about the areas.'

The squeeze inside was so unexpected it made him jolt. He should be jumping for joy. But he strangely wasn't.

Sitting in the flickering firelight with Bonnie, watching the orange light glint off her auburn hair and light up her pale skin, giving her advice to leave seemed ridiculous.

It was just the two of them right now. In the glimmering light her bright blue eyes reflected off his. He was close enough to see the tiny freckles across the bridge of her nose.

But he wanted to be closer.

He licked his dry lips and watched as she mirrored his actions. This woman was going to drive him crazy.

'Where?' His voice was so low it was barely audible.

'One rental in Olderfield, one in Rancor and the flat is in Calderwood.' She named the prices for each.

He shook his head. 'Olderfield is not an area you want to stay in.' It was almost a relief to say those words. 'The price of the rental in Rancor is nearly three hundred pounds a month above any other. It sounds like a bit of a con. As for Calderwood—it's nice. It's fine. But it's the other side of the city. You'd need to change Freya's school again. Do you really want to do that?'

Everything he was saying was safe and rational. It was sensible.

But that wasn't how he was feeling right now.

He'd inched closer. And so had she.

It was almost as if an invisible force were drawing them together. Pushing them together. He could feel her warm breath dancing across his skin. The scent she'd put on after showering was pervading its way around him, wrapping round like a tentacle and reeling him in.

He had absolutely no wish or desire to resist it. None at all.

He was trying to read what was in her eyes. He was sure he could see passion burning there. She hadn't moved; she hadn't flinched. She just unobtrusively moved even closer, slotting under his arm as though she were meant to be there.

And for the first time it felt as if someone *was* meant to be there.

The flickering fire didn't just bathe the room and her

skin in warm light. It made him feel different inside. It made him feel that the thing that was missing from this home might finally be there.

There was no time for talk.

He moved forwards, his lips against hers.

It was the lightest of touches. The merest hint of what was to come.

She let out a little sigh and her hand moved up to his shoulder, as if she was going to pull him closer.

The tiny voice came out of nowhere, cutting through the building heat in the room.

'Mummy?'

They sprang apart. Both of them realising what had almost happened. Bonnie was on her feet in an instant and out of the door, running up the stairs to the little voice at the top of them.

Jacob was left in the room. His breathing ragged and his soul twisting like the ugly black mark on the wall. Was he mad?

What had he nearly done? She was a colleague. For a few minutes he'd completely forgotten about the little girl upstairs.

What could have happened next?

He stood up and flicked on the light, flooding the room with a bright white glare and dousing the flames in an instant.

It was time to pretend this had never happened.

CHAPTER SIX

'WOW, WHAT'S GOING on with Jacob Layton?' Kerry came through the theatre doors and walked to the sink, scrubbing her hands post-surgery.

Bonnie glanced over her shoulder as Isabel walked out of the theatre doors too, ripping off her gloves and gown and joining Kerry at the sink. 'I know.' The two of them exchanged glances and smiled at each other. 'I wonder what's changed his mood.'

Isabel's eyes met Bonnie's and an uncomfortable shiver went down her spine. 'What are you talking about?' she asked.

Kerry rolled her eyes. 'I dropped an instrument tray in Theatre. Usually, Jacob would have gone nuts and I'd have been flung out of Theatre.'

'Really?' Bonnie frowned. She'd heard of surgeons being extreme in Theatre. But she'd never experienced it herself. She certainly didn't like the thought of one of the obstetricians she worked with behaving like that. She wouldn't stand for it.

But Isabel and Kerry were still smiling at her as they finished drying their hands. 'What's that Scottish word you use to describe people who are grumpy or miserable?'

Bonnie was a bit unsure where this was going. 'Crabbit.' She used it quite a lot, along with a whole host of other Scottish words that were second nature to her, but seemed to leave the staff baffled.

Isabel and Kerry exchanged smiles again. Isabel deposited her paper towels in the bin. 'It's a good word. A very descriptive word.' She turned to her colleague. 'Kerry, would you say that Jacob's been crabbit lately?'

Kerry crossed the room. 'Nope. I'd say Jacob's had a whole new personality transplant. He didn't shout at all today. He just looked up and asked me to get him a new set of instruments. The whole Theatre was shocked.'

Bonnie frowned. 'Jacob normally behaved like that in Theatre?'

Isabel laughed. 'Not just Theatre. Labour suite, wards, clinics, the neonatal unit.' She held up her hand. 'Don't get me wrong, he would always switch on the charm for the patients, but for the staff?' She shook her head. 'Oh, no.'

Kerry put her hands on her hips. 'And both of you ladies haven't been here that long. A few years ago, Jacob was always Doctor Charming. But then just over a year ago he changed—practically overnight. He's been like a bear with a sore head ever since. Or he had been...' she turned to face Bonnie '...until a few weeks ago.'

Bonnie shifted uncomfortably on her feet. Two pairs of eyes were staring at her, smiling. 'I have no idea what you mean.'

Isabel walked past and tapped her on the shoulder. 'I don't know what it is you're doing. But all I can say is— keep doing it.'

Kerry nodded in agreement as the doors swung open again. It was Sean, the new obstetrician who'd arrived from Melbourne just a few weeks before Bonnie. 'Hi, ladies, sorry to interrupt. Isabel, can we talk?'

Something flickered across Isabel's face. It was the

strangest look Bonnie had seen in a while. She couldn't quite put her finger on it. Something between complete avoidance and dread. It seemed that Jess Black had been right.

Isabel was super friendly and completely confident about the work she did. This was the first time that Bonnie had seen her look neither.

'It will only take a few minutes, Isabel.' Sean looked tired, but it seemed he wasn't going to be put off.

Her eyes flitted over to Bonnie. 'Didn't you want me to see a patient on the labour suite?'

'Eh…yes.' Bonnie knew avoidance tactics when she saw them. And there was no way she wasn't going to help out a colleague. Particularly when this might take the heat off her.

In a way it was good that people thought Jacob was more amenable. The question was—what had been wrong with him before? She had no idea. She and her daughter were living with a guy they hardly knew. She'd almost kissed him the other night! If Freya hadn't shouted…

She was crazy. She was plainly crazy. Jacob was her boss. Her brand-new boss. The last thing she should be doing on this planet was kissing the boss—no matter how much she'd wanted to.

She bit her lip. She was new here. She hadn't even had time to find her feet yet. Her new job was a big responsibility. *That* was where she should be focusing her attention.

She had Freya to think about. Her little girl had already been exposed to one disastrous relationship—there was no way she wanted to expose her to another. It was too soon. Far too soon.

It was time to focus on work—and only work. She

wouldn't allow thoughts of Jacob to distract her from her job.

Sean disappeared back out of the doors, sighing loudly. Isabel's eyes flickered towards Bonnie. 'Thanks,' she said before putting her head down and disappearing out of another door.

Kerry folded her arms across her chest. 'This place just gets more interesting by the second.'

Bonnie gave a little smile and shake of her head as she headed to the door. 'Kerry, you have no idea.'

Jacob was feeling strangely nervous. One of the other obstetricians had been off sick for a few days and he'd covered their on-call rota. It meant that he and Bonnie hadn't really been alone together for the last few days.

The front room was back to normal. The walls freshly painted and bright white again. Except, the room wasn't back to normal. The room had changed. And the mood of the house had changed with it.

The temperature seemed to have dropped permanently in the last few days. It meant that every time he walked through the front door of his house, his feet turned automatically to the fireplace in the front room.

Bonnie was right. There was something about a fireplace. He was drawn to it like the proverbial moth to a flame. Last night he'd even contemplated buying a rug to put in front of it. He'd never really thought about soft furnishings before. He wasn't that kind of guy. He was all about the basics. The functional stuff.

Except that last night he'd spent an hour on the Internet wondering what colour rug to buy.

Now his fingers hovered over something else. Freya had been really excited the other night when she'd seen the advert for the latest kids' Christmas film. It had been years since Jacob had gone to the movies. He'd still been in his early twenties.

He glanced at the film times before clicking to buy tickets. It was Tuesday night. Freya and Bonnie didn't do anything on a Tuesday. Monday was dancing, Wednesday was Rainbow Brownies. He couldn't believe that after a few weeks he actually knew this kind of stuff. It was all so alien to him.

Once he'd bought the tickets he looked for a restaurant. For the first time in his life, Jacob Layton picked up the phone to ask if his favourite place to eat had a children's menu. It had never crossed his mind before.

It was odd. This wasn't a date. This wasn't anything like that.

He just wanted to have some time away from the hospital, away from the house, and to spend a little time with Bonnie and Freya.

He was planning. He was being rational. But little voices in his brain were screaming at him. He didn't do this kind of stuff. Well, of course, he'd taken a woman to dinner before. The truth was he'd done that on *lots* of occasions. But incorporating a child into his plans? This was a whole new concept for him.

Bonnie appeared at the door. 'Jacob? Outpatients just phoned. Lisa Brennan, a thirty-three-year-old diabetic who is in for her twenty-week scan. They're having a few problems and wondered if you could go down. The sonographer is new and thinks there may be an anomaly but isn't quite sure.'

He stood up straight away. 'No problem. I'll go now.' He paused in the doorway. 'I thought maybe we could do something tonight?'

A look of mild panic flickered across Bonnie's face and his stomach dropped. 'I mean, you, me and Freya.

I was thinking about that new film she wanted to see. What do you think?'

He was babbling now. Doing the thing that he found so endearing in Bonnie. Why had she looked panicked? Did she really want to say no? Maybe he was reading things all wrong.

Her lips pressed together and after a few seconds the edges turned upwards. 'Freya would love that. It's a great idea.'

He brushed past her. 'Good. I'll book tickets and maybe we could grab some dinner first?'

He kept walking down the corridor as she gave the slightest nod of her head. He didn't want to tell her he'd already booked the tickets and the restaurant. That would seem presumptuous.

It was the oddest feeling. Jacob hadn't felt this nervous asking a girl out since he was a teenager. For a second, he'd thought she might actually say no.

As he turned the corner at the bottom of the corridor Bonnie was still standing at the office door with a smile on her face.

For a second he felt sixteen again. It was all he could do not to punch the air.

Bonnie was nervous—and that was ridiculous. She looked at the clothes laid out on her bed. Nothing seemed to suit.

'Wear the Christmas jumper, Mummy!' said Freya as she bounced in the room. 'We can match.'

Bonnie blinked. Freya hadn't been wearing that jumper a few minutes ago. She was going through a stage of changing her clothes constantly—and putting everything she'd worn for ten minutes in the washing basket.

She smiled. 'Well, I suppose it is officially December

now.' She pulled the black jumper, adorned with a bright green Christmas tree and glittering red sequins for the Christmas baubles, over her head. As soon as she pulled it on she felt more comfortable.

That was what was wrong. She was fretting over what to wear as if this were actually a *date*. And it wasn't. But it had felt like that when Jacob had asked her. It had given her that warm, tingly feeling that spread throughout her body and stayed there all day.

Ridiculous. This was Jacob being polite and taking out his house guests. And if there hadn't been that soft, sizzling kiss a few nights ago that might have been a rational thought. It might have been brief but she couldn't get the feel of Jacob's lips out of her mind.

'Come on, Mummy.' Bonnie pulled on her favourite jeans and stuck her feet into her boots. She'd put make-up on this morning and had no wish to do it again, so just reapplied some lipstick. There. Ready.

Jacob was waiting for them at the bottom of the stairs as they walked down. The look of appreciation and smile he gave her made the little fire inside light up again.

'I can't wait to see this film,' chattered Freya. 'Three people at school have seen it already and they said it's brilliant. The princess dances on ice and the prince lives underneath the water.'

'Are you sure you're up for this?' Bonnie asked.

But he smiled. 'Oh, I'm sure. I'm sure in the next few days every adult will have seen this film too and it's all we'll hear about.' He opened the front door. 'I booked Paulette's Italian. Are you okay with that? I thought it would suit Freya since spaghetti bolognaise is her favourite food.'

She'd expected to go to the nearest fast-food restaurant. Jacob Layton was proving to be more than a little surprising.

It only took ten minutes to reach the cinema complex and the nearby restaurant. Dinner was almost a disaster. Freya was too excited to eat and ended up wearing most of her spaghetti rather than eating it. But the food was good and the company even better.

Jacob was careful not to talk shop in front of Freya—or ask Bonnie any difficult questions about being back in Scotland. He asked Freya about school and her friends, and Bonnie about her favourite things and how she was settling in.

She took a sip of her glass of wine. 'I love CRMU. The staff are really friendly. A few of them have invited me out—Isabel, Hope and Jessica. But it's difficult. If we were still at home I could ask my mum and dad to babysit. Going out in the evenings in Cambridge isn't re-ally an option for me.'

Jacob hesitated. His fork poised just before his mouth. 'I could do it.'

She almost choked. 'What? No, I couldn't ask you to do that.'

'I mean, as long as I wasn't on call or anything. I mean, once Freya's had dinner and done her homework, there's really no problem. We could watch a film together and then it would be time for bed.'

Bonnie shook her head, glancing sideways at Freya, who seemed to have missed the conversation. 'That's so kind of you to offer. But no, Jacob, I wouldn't do that to you.' She paused for a second. 'I could always ask Lynn, the childminder. I'm sure she would say it was okay.' She put her hand around Freya's shoulder. 'But I'm just not ready to do that yet. We've had a lot of change in a short period of time. I'd like her to feel really settled before I start thinking about going out.'

Jacob nodded thoughtfully then shrugged. 'Okay. But the offer is there if you need it.'

'Is it time for the film yet?' cut in Freya, smiling, with her bolognaise-smeared face.

Bonnie glanced at her watch as she wiped Freya's face with a napkin. 'I think it is. Are you ready to go?'

Freya bounced out of her seat. 'I'm ready. Let's go and see the princess.'

Jacob paid their bill and helped Freya on with her jacket before they walked the short distance to the cinema. It was already busy, with numerous excitable children all waiting to see the film. The noise level was incredible.

Jacob winced. 'Is every kids' show like this?'

Bonnie nodded. 'Believe it or not, they do go quiet when the film starts.'

They collected their tickets and bought some popcorn, then filed into the cinema and found their seats. Freya changed seats three times. Sitting between them, then on one side of Bonnie, on one side of Jacob and back to the middle again. She leaned forwards as the film started.

In the darkness of the cinema something struck Bonnie. Freya had never been to the cinema with her father. Robert had always managed to find an excuse not to go on family outings with them and the cinema had rapidly become a treat for Bonnie and Freya on their own.

This was the first time she'd actually been at the cinema with a man since she'd been born. Regret twisted inside Bonnie. She should have chosen better. Robert had never lived up to the role of a father, and now here was Jacob, a single man with no experience of kids, bending over backwards to be accommodating towards them.

She wasn't sure what all this meant, but it was so nice to feel considered. She appreciated it more than she could ever say.

She reached over in the darkness, across the space where Freya leaned forwards, and slid her hand into Jacob's. He turned towards her, surprise on his face.

'Thank you for doing this,' she whispered.

He smiled and gave her hand a squeeze, circling his thumb in her palm.

He kept it that way for the whole ninety-minute film. And she let him.

CHAPTER SEVEN

THE HOUSE WAS looking truly magical. Freya was watching from the window, the excitement almost too much for her.

Today had been a quiet day. It was odd. It was a few days into December already and there were still no decorations in the house. Bonnie had always been the type to put her decorations up on the first of the month. Any later made her antsy.

Yesterday, a few tree decorations had arrived that she'd ordered online. Along with a personalised stocking for Freya and some Christmas candles.

This morning she'd had a look in some of the cupboards around the house, expecting to find a few cardboard boxes of decorations that she and Freya could put up. But there was nothing. Not even a single strand of tinsel.

Maybe Jacob hadn't bothered because he lived alone? He'd already told her he worked at the hospital most Christmases. He'd made a few fleeting remarks about not really doing Christmas. But nothing definite. Nothing that he'd actually explained.

So, this morning she and Freya had hatched the master plan. Jacob was working today. It was a Saturday and there were a few patients in the hospital that needed to be reviewed, so she was sure he would be kept busy.

It gave her and Freya time to visit the local hardware store and stock up on Christmas decorations. The kind that she'd always wanted to buy. Her credit card had trembled as she'd entered the store and fainted on the way out.

She'd never bought a real tree before. But the hardware store could deliver on the same day, and only an hour after they'd left the store the delivery driver arrived. He was great. He carried the tree up the front steps and into the front room. It had already been mounted for them and he made sure it was straight before he left.

Freya had been jumping for joy as they'd plugged the twinkling star lights in to check they worked before winding them around the tree. By four o'clock it was already starting to get dark. Bonnie pulled the blinds in the front room. She didn't want Jacob to see the tree from the street. She wanted him to come through the front door and get the full effect.

A thick green and red garland was wound up the banister on the stairs. Another, set with red twinkling lights, was adorning the mantelpiece in the front room. The fire was burning in the hearth and she'd switched off the main lights so only the twinkling lights and flickering flames warmed the room.

Freya wound her hands around Bonnie's neck. 'It's so beautiful, isn't it, Mummy?'

'Yes, honey, it is.'

She so wanted Christmas to be perfect for her daughter. It was beginning to look as if they wouldn't have found somewhere else to stay by then. Her ex hadn't even tried to make contact with his daughter—not even once—since they'd moved down here.

It was no real surprise. He hadn't bothered when they'd stayed in the same town. But she was worried about the effect on her little girl. How must it feel for Freya to know her daddy didn't love her? Not the way he should.

They finished unpacking the last of the deliveries. A carved wooden nativity scene that Freya helped set out on one of the side tables. Everything really did look perfect.

She heard a car door slam outside and Freya ran and peeked under the blinds. 'Jacob's coming. He's coming, Mummy.' She jumped up and down on the spot clapping her hands.

Bonnie couldn't wipe the smile off her face. She stood in the corridor, just at the entrance to the front room— waiting for him to appear.

It only took a few seconds. He walked through the front door, dropping his case and hanging his jacket on the coat stand.

'Hey, Jacob.' She smiled.

He smiled back. 'Hey, yourself,' then started to frown. He gave a little start, his eyes fixed on the banister behind her.

'We've got a surprise,' yelled Freya, running through the door.

Bonnie's skin prickled, her hairs standing on end. He didn't look happy. He didn't look anything *like* happy. Her blood felt as if it were running cold.

All of a sudden she got the feeling that she'd done something very wrong.

Jacob strode past her and into the front room, virtually ignoring Freya.

His face fell as soon as he walked into the middle of the floor, holding his hands out as he spun around, taking in the full effect of the room. She loved it. It was beautiful and really captured the spirit of Christmas with the flickering flames and twinkling festive lights.

Anyone would love it.

Anyone but Jacob, that was.

He looked as if he'd just been sat down in his worst possible nightmare. He walked over to the fireplace and tugged harshly on the beautiful green and red garland, pulling part of it free. 'What on earth have you done?' His voice was incredulous. 'Tell me you're joking. You've done this everywhere? This?'

He stared at the greenery in his hand, then dropped it to the floor. Freya's mouth was hanging open. She was stunned—as was Bonnie—but, what was more, she looked a little frightened.

He walked over and grabbed the tree, knocking some of the carefully hung red and green ornaments to the floor, one of them breaking with a crash. 'Who on earth said you could do this? What made you think you could decorate my house without my permission?' In a surge of anger he pushed the tree to the floor, scattering the decorations everywhere and making the lights flicker dangerously.

He was furious. Really furious. So angry he was trembling. Bonnie had never, ever seen Jacob like this. And although she was bewildered, she wasn't afraid; in fact, she was angry. But he wasn't finished. He leaned over the fallen Christmas tree and started yanking the tinsel from it. The harshness of his movements meant the sitting-room air and floor quickly filled with tiny ripped-off strands of multicoloured tinsel all around them. 'I hate this. I have to tolerate this stuff everywhere else—but not in my house!'

She walked over and put her arm around Freya's shoulder. 'What is wrong with you, Jacob? We wanted to do something nice for you—to surprise you.'

But it was almost as if he hadn't heard her. He was still shaking his head at the twinkling lights. He crossed the room and flicked the switch on one of the plugs, plunging that part of the room into darkness.

Almost as dark as your mood was her fleeting thought as he turned on her again.

'How dare you do this? Didn't I tell you I don't celebrate Christmas? I don't even *like* Christmas.' The words were said with such venom she actually found herself pulling back a little. But it only lasted a second. Because after that the red mist started to descend.

All the hours of work and preparation. The build-up of excitement between her and Freya all day. And he was ruining it all with some angry words and some hand movements. Destroying all their hard work.

She dropped her arm from around Freya's shoulder and stepped right up to his face. 'Oh, I get that. I get that you don't like Christmas. Enough, Jacob!' she snapped. 'You've made your point. You don't like Christmas. Well, pardon me for not being a mind reader. And pardon me, and my daughter, for trying to do something to say thank you for letting us stay. We won't make that mistake again!'

She turned at the sound of a little sob behind her and dropped to her knees, wrapping her arms around Freya's little body. She would kill him. She would kill him with her bare hands for his pathetic overreaction.

Jacob flinched. It was as if reality had just slapped him on the forehead and he realised the impact his reactions had had on Freya. For the tiniest second he seemed to hesitate, but Bonnie glared at him, furious with him for upsetting her daughter, and he spun on his heel and stalked back along the corridor, slamming the front door behind him.

The blood was pounding in her ears. She'd never been so angry with someone—not even her pathetic husband when she'd found him in bed with her so-called friend. Freya's shoulders were shaking and her head was buried into the nape of Bonnie's neck.

Over Christmas decorations? Really?

She didn't care that this was his house. She didn't care that on every other occasion Jacob had been a kind and hospitable housemate. This blew everything else out of the water.

He'd upset her daughter.

Jacob Layton was about to find out that hell hath no fury like an angry mother.

'Isn't it about time you went home?'

He lifted his head from the bar and the barman gestured his head towards the clock. The guy obviously wanted to close up.

The old guy shrugged. 'Can't be that bad.'

Jacob picked up the now-warm remnants of beer and washed them down. 'You have no idea.'

He looked out through the murky window. It had started to snow. He didn't even have a jacket. In his haste to leave the house he hadn't stopped to pick one up.

How far had he walked? He had no idea. He'd never even been in this pub before. Let alone nearly fallen asleep at the bar.

He gave the barman a little nod and shivered as he walked out of the door and the wind whistled around his thin jumper. With his suit trousers and business shoes it was hardly winter gear. But he hadn't stopped to think about much before he left.

That was the trouble. He *couldn't* think. He'd taken one look at all those Christmas decorations and a whole host of unwanted memories had come flooding back.

It was ridiculous. It was pathetic. He'd spent every year of his life around Christmas decorations.

But not in his space. Not in his home. In other places, they were bearable. In other places there were other things to do, other things to think about. At home, they would be right under his nose constantly—forcing him to think about things he'd long since pushed to the back of his mind.

The cold wind started to penetrate through his thin jumper, making him shiver. His insides were cringing.

Freya.

Her little face had crumpled and she'd started to cry.

He was ashamed of himself. Ashamed of his behaviour. He hadn't even stopped to think about her. And everything about that was wrong.

What embarrassed him even more was the fact that if it had been just Bonnie, he might not be feeling so ashamed. It had taken a five-year-old to teach him what acceptable behaviour was. What kind of human being did that make him?

The kind that had spent the last three hours in a bar, like some sad and lonely old drifter sitting on a bar stool alone, nursing one bottle of beer after another.

Pathetic. Was that really the kind of man he wanted to be? Was that the kind of man that would have made his mother proud?

All of a sudden he wasn't feeling the cold any more. All of sudden he was lost in distant memories as his feet trudged through the snow, his dress shoes getting damper by the second as the memories of his mother burned deep in his mind.

She had complemented his closed-off father beautifully with her calming good nature. She was always able to put a smile on his father's often grumpy face, or give a measured argument against his forceful opinions—skills that Jacob hadn't seemed to inherit.

If his mother had still been alive he would never have ended up at loggerheads with his father over his refusal to follow the family tradition into the military. His mother would have argued peacefully, but successfully, for his entry to medical school and the opportunity to pursue his own career options.

His father had never really accepted his decision—particularly when Jacob had opted to become an obstetrician. It wasn't heroic enough for his father. It wasn't front line enough, or pioneering enough. He didn't see the joy in bringing life into the world, compared with so many other specialities that frequently dealt with death. Just as well his mother had left him enough money, not only to put himself through medical school, but also to allow him the freedom to place a deposit on a house and have the option of being part of one of the finest universities and hospitals in the country.

She *would* be proud of him. She *should* be proud of him. She would love what her son had achieved.

But she would also expect him to treat everyone with the same respect he'd given her. With the love and compassion he'd given her.

The long street ahead was coated with snow. The orange streetlights cast a warm glow across the snow-topped cars. People spilled out of the pub ahead of him, laughing and joking. Full of cheer.

When was the last time he'd been in Cambridge city centre on a Saturday night? He couldn't even remember. Now he looked around him, Christmas was everywhere. Every shop window was decorated and a few of the flats on the main street had glistening trees in their windows.

He hung his head as the cold bit harder. Festive cheer.

It should be spreading warmth through his soul. What on earth was he going home to?

His footsteps quickened as a horrible thought shot through his head. What if they'd left? What if they'd left because of his behaviour?

The beer sloshed around in his stomach. He hadn't eaten at all in the last few hours and that last thought made him feel physically sick.

The thought of going home to an empty house after a month wasn't at all appealing. It was strange how things had changed without him really noticing. *Please don't let them leave.* He would much prefer it if Bonnie was waiting at home ready to tell him exactly what she thought of him. He could take it.

He might even try and explain why he'd behaved like that—if, of course, she gave him a chance to speak.

The snow was getting heavier. It was kicking up under his feet and lying on his shoulders and eyelashes. His feet moved even quicker. How far had he walked?

It was a relief to finally turn into his street. Only a few windows were uncovered, letting their warm light spill out onto the snow-covered street. From a distance, he could see his tightly pulled white blinds.

He swallowed. His mouth had never felt so dry. Drinking beer certainly hadn't helped. More than anything right now he just wanted to know what lay behind his door.

He had to stop himself from breaking into a run. His brain was spinning. What would he do if they'd left? What would he say if they'd stayed? A thousand excuses and explanations were running through his brain. But somehow he knew they wouldn't wash with Bonnie.

Nothing but the truth would do for her.

He pulled his key from his pocket as he walked up the

steps. He paused at the door. The house was silent. Not a single sound from inside.

The traditional door handle was icy cold. He pushed down on it and the door clicked open.

Relief. Pure and utter relief. If Bonnie had left, the door would have been locked.

He brushed the snow off his shoulders and hair and kicked it from his damp shoes.

Still nothing.

He walked silently down the corridor. The light was out in the kitchen and in the back sitting room. His stomach twisted. The green and red garland was gone from the stairs. There was no sign it had even been there.

He held his breath as he stepped into his front room. His completely bare front room.

All signs of Christmas were gone.

The tree. The lights. The garland. The nativity.

Just one small lamp was lit in the corner of the room, reflecting the bare white walls back at him. He'd never realised just how sparse this room was.

Bonnie was sitting on the sofa. She didn't even turn her head towards him. She was staring at the now unlit fire. Her jaw was set. In one hand she held a glass of wine, the fingers of the other hand running up and down the stem of the glass.

He braced himself, but she said nothing.

'Bonnie,' he acknowledged. An elephant had just decided to sit on his chest. At least that was what it felt like.

She didn't move, didn't flinch. It was almost as if he weren't even there.

He swallowed again. He really, really needed a drink of water. His mouth had never felt so dry. But he took a deep breath and sat down next to her on the sofa.

'Let me try and explain,' he said quietly.

'Oh, you'd better.' Her words dripped ice. Any minute now she was going to pick up the bottle of wine at her feet and launch it at his head.

Jacob had never really been lost for words before. This was a first for him. He didn't talk. He didn't share. Ever since his father had packed him off to boarding school once his mother died, there just hadn't been anyone to share with. Not like that. Not like the way he used to with her.

The truth was, he always felt that no one else had ever been that invested in him. Building walls around yourself as a child protected you as an adult. At least, that was what he'd always thought.

His behaviour tonight had been over the top. He had to explain. He hated what she might think of him right now. What Freya might think of him right now.

'I'm sorry I upset Freya tonight. I never meant to do that.'

'Well, you did. And it will be the first and last time.'

Bonnie's voice had no hesitation. The line was very clearly drawn in the sand.

'Let me be clear. Freya is my first and *only* priority. Every. Single. Day.'

He could feel prickles down his back. She was worse than mad.

'I know that.'

He leaned back against the sofa. This was going to take some work. He wasn't used to talking about himself. And he had no idea what Bonnie's response might be to his words.

For a tiny second he squeezed his eyes shut. They were still here. That must mean something.

He licked his dry lips. 'I haven't told you much about my past.'

Her fingers continued to stroke up and down the wine-glass stem. It was almost as if she was using it as a measure of control. 'No. You haven't.'

She was wearing those jeans again and a soft woollen jumper. Right now he wanted to reach out and touch her. Right now he wanted to feel some comfort. Saying these words out loud wasn't easy.

'My mother died when I was ten.'

There. It was out there. The light in the corner flickered inexplicably and he heard her suck in a breath.

'She was the heart of our family. I was an only child and my father spent most of his life in the military. When my mother died it was almost as if all the life was just sucked out of us both.'

She turned a little towards him. 'What did you do?'

He shrugged. 'What could I do? I was ten. I'd spent most of my time with my mother. We'd shared everything. My relationship with my father had always been a little strained. I just think he didn't know how to relate to kids.'

As he was talking he'd moved to face her and as he finished his last sentence her eyebrows lifted. He knew exactly what she was thinking. Like father, like son. And he was struck by the realisation that was the last thing he wanted.

He fixed on her blue eyes. 'My dad sent me to boarding school.'

'Do those places even exist any more? I thought they only ever existed in Enid Blyton books.'

He shook his head. 'Oh, they exist all right. And they're just the place to send a ten-year-old whose mother's died.' He couldn't keep the irony or the bitterness out of his voice. 'I hated every second of it. The education part was fine. The school activity part was fine. But to go from living with your mother, to living there, with nothing really in between...' His voice tailed off.

'Why did he send you there?'

Jacob sighed. 'There was no one else to look after me. I'm an only child and so were my father and mother. Both sets of grandparents were already dead. My father had another posting abroad with the military and there was no question that he wouldn't go. He told me later that he'd always planned on sending me to boarding school.' He pushed up the sleeves of his wet jumper.

She tilted her head to one side. 'Had your mother stopped that?'

He shook his head. 'I have no idea.' He groaned and sagged back against the sofa. 'There were so many things that I wished I had asked her. So many conversations I wish I could remember. Most of it is just all caught up in here.' He waved his finger next to his head. 'Sometimes I think that things I remember I've just made up.'

'How did she die?'

Jacob hesitated, then took a deep breath. 'Cancer. Non-Hodgkin's lymphoma. It was brutal—it sucked the life right out of her.'

She licked her lips. 'Did you go to your mother's funeral?'

He nodded. 'It was full of people I didn't really know. No one really spoke to me. And because of the time of year it was bitter cold and lashing with rain. We were only at the graveside for around five minutes.'

A little spark of realisation shot across her face. 'When did your mother die, Jacob?'

This was it. This was the important part. He felt his eyes fill up and was instantly embarrassed. Men didn't cry. Men *shouldn't* cry.

But no matter how hard he tried not to, one tear escaped and slid down his cheek. His voice was hoarse. 'She died three days before Christmas. I came home to a house we'd decorated together, that would never feel the same again.'

'Oh, Jacob.' Bonnie's tears fell instantly, and she reached up to his cheek to brush his away. 'I can't even begin to imagine what that felt like.'

Now he'd started he couldn't stop. He felt safe. He felt safe talking to Bonnie. Someone he'd known only a month and invited into his home. There was nothing superficial about Bonnie Reid. She was all heart and soul. He'd never met anyone like her before. Or if he had, he'd never taken the time to get to know them.

It felt right to tell Bonnie about his mother and why his insides were so messed up about Christmas.

'I felt like when we buried my mother, we buried a little bit of ourselves. My father was never the same. I can't remember ever seeing my father smile once my mother died. Our relationship was non-existent. I'm embarrassed by it. I've no idea if he just couldn't cope. If it was all just grief. Or, if my mother had brought out another side of him, and when she died he just reverted back to how he normally was. All I know is that from the age of ten, happiness just didn't feature in our house.'

Bonnie's tears were free-flowing. 'That's awful. You had no one? No one else you could turn to?'

He shook his head. 'Christmas felt like a curse after that. That's why I hate it so much. I try not to be bitter. But it just doesn't evoke the happy memories in me that it does for others. I do have good memories of Christmases with my mother. But they were so long ago. Sometimes I wonder if they even existed.'

'Oh, Jacob.' Bonnie reached over, her hand stroking

the top of his. She left it there and squeezed gently, the warm sleeve of her jumper touching his forearm.

It was the touch. The heat of her hand, coupled with the act of compassion. Something he hadn't felt in such a long time. Or maybe it was the relief?

The relief of reaching thirty-seven and finally being able to share with someone. It was as if a whole dark weight had lifted off his shoulders. He couldn't rationalise it. It didn't make any sense. But saying the words out loud, to someone who might actually understand, was a whole new concept for Jacob.

These last fourteen months had been so hard. The next few weeks probably the hardest while he waited for his results. The outcome of whether he'd come out the other side of non-Hodgkin's lymphoma, or he'd succumb like his mother. Bonnie and Freya had been good for him. They'd brought some light back into his life at a time when he needed it most.

Bonnie squeezed his hand again. 'You can't do that, Jacob. You can't take your feelings out on my little girl.'

He pulled his hand away and put them both up to his face, cringing. 'I know that. I'm so sorry. I wasn't thinking straight. I just came in, saw the decorations and it brought back a whole host of things I just wasn't ready for.' He put his head in his hands for a second. 'I overreacted. I *know* I overreacted. I'm sorry, I really am.' He turned to face her.

She was beautiful. Bonnie Reid was actually beautiful. Even with the harsh light in this stark white room, her dark red hair, bright blue eyes and pale skin made her the most beautiful woman he'd ever been close to. 'What can I do? What can I do to make it up to her? To make it up to you? I don't want her to hate me. I don't want her to be scared of me.'

Bonnie nodded slowly and met his gaze. There was a gentle smile on her lips. 'I can't tell you that, Jacob. You've got to figure that out for yourself. You're the adult—she's the child. You have to take some time to work through how you feel about everything.'

'How do I do that?' His voice was low. He couldn't tear his eyes away from her. All he wanted to do was reach out and touch her perfect skin—to join the invisible dots between the light sprinkling of freckles across her nose.

He wanted Bonnie and Freya to feel safe. To feel safe around him. Just as he'd felt safe to tell her about his past.

'What happened to your dad?'

He gave a little sigh. 'He died—two years ago of heart failure. Had a funeral with full military honours.' He raised his eyebrows. 'He would have been very proud.'

Bonnie bent down and lifted the bottle of wine. 'Why don't we have a drink together and just talk?'

He nodded, then smiled as he took the bottle from her hand and turned the label around. He raised his eyebrows. 'Did you open the most expensive bottle of wine that I had?'

She smiled and held up her phone. 'You bet your life I did. I looked it up online first. I was planning on finishing it before you got back. You're lucky I left you any.' She handed him a glass.

He poured the remaining wine into his glass and stopped for a minute, holding it between both hands. He was staring at the liquid in the glass. 'I'm just glad that you didn't leave,' he said quietly.

She reached over and put a hand on his back. 'I wanted to. I didn't even care that we had nowhere to go.' She shook her head, as if she couldn't quite understand herself. 'But I just couldn't, Jacob. Not like this.'

There was a silence for a few moments between them. Was she considering the same implications that he was? That what had started out as a temporary arrangement was becoming so much more?

He looked up through heavy lids. Now he'd come in from the cold, the heat of the house was hitting him in a big way. He'd gone from being frozen to the bone to feeling superheated in a matter of minutes.

Sensations of fatigue were sweeping over him. But his body was fighting it every step of the way. Fighting to hold on to the other sensations in his prickling skin. Those bright blue eyes were mesmerising. She didn't need to speak. It was almost as if he knew what she was thinking. Was he imagining this? He'd never felt a connection like this before.

'I guess not everyone leaves,' he whispered.

Bonnie took a long, slow breath and put her wine glass on the floor. Although her actions were slow and measured, he didn't doubt for a second that she knew exactly what she was doing.

As she turned to face him, one leg was pulled up on the sofa, tucking under her as she put her arms around his neck. 'No, Jacob,' she whispered. 'Not everyone leaves.'

His breath was stuck somewhere in his throat. He'd never told anyone what he'd just told Bonnie. Now she seemed connected to him—tied to him, and he didn't want that to end. The blood was roaring through his ears. The feel of the soft fluffy wool on the sleeves of her jumper pushed his temperature skyward.

But his self-defence mechanisms were still kicking into place. He'd lived his life too long like this for them to disappear instantly. 'But you did leave,' he murmured. 'You left your husband.'

He was fixed on her eyes. Fixed on the perfectness

of her skin and beautiful auburn hair framing her face. She nodded. 'I did.' It was almost as if she sensed she had to tease him every part of the way. She gave a little smile, 'But I had exceptional circumstances—you know what they were.'

He reached over and touched her hair. 'Not really. Tell me about them. Tell me about Freya's dad.'

He could see her hesitation, see her sucking in a breath. He'd just shared with her. She now knew about one of the biggest influencing factors in his life. He'd barely scratched the surface with her.

Her eyes fixed on the floor. 'Robert was my boyfriend. We were together about a year when I fell pregnant unexpectedly.' She threw up her hands. 'I know. Don't say anything. A midwife accidentally falling pregnant. The irony kills me.' Then she smiled. 'But Freya is the best accident that will ever happen to me.' She bit her lip. 'It's stupid really, and hindsight is a wonderful thing. Robert's parents were real traditionalists. So we got swept along with their ideals and got married before Freya arrived. The truth was Robert was never really the marrying kind.'

'But you married him anyway?' He gave a little smile. It wasn't really a question, it was a more a sympathetic observation. Bonnie didn't seem upset, just a little sad.

She started winding a strand of hair around her finger. She nodded. 'I think I was more in love with the *idea* of being in love, than actually *being* in love. In my heart of hearts, I never really pictured us growing old together.'

'And?'

She shrugged her shoulders. 'I was busy with work and juggling childcare for Freya. I kind of lost sight of being married. Robert was distant—distracted. I suspected something was going on. It made me mad. I came home early from work one day and found another car in the drive. I let myself into the house and found Freya playing downstairs. Robert was upstairs, in bed, with one of my closest friends.' She shook her head and sagged back a little. 'It wasn't my finest hour. The fact Freya was in the house. The fact it was one of my friends…'

Jacob raised his eyebrows. 'Oh, no. What did you do?'

She rolled her eyes. 'My "friend" ended up naked in my front garden after I'd marched her down the stairs. Robert's clothes were deposited out of the bedroom window—so at least she found something to wear.' She shook her head. 'After that, I just grabbed some things for me and Freya, packed up and went to my parents. I filed for divorce straight away.'

He was watching her closely. 'How did you feel?'

She paused for a second. 'It's probably a really awful thing to say—but I was more humiliated than anything else. Robert and I had been growing apart. I probably always thought we would come to a natural end. I just didn't expect it to be like that.' She gave a rueful smile. 'I wasn't exactly heartbroken about it. I might even have been secretly relieved it was over. But we lived in a small place. Every person in the town knew exactly what Robert had done to me. And pride is a terrible thing. I felt people staring at me wherever I went. I couldn't take it any longer.'

He nodded slowly. 'So you came to Cambridge?'

'I had to. I know you understand, Jacob. It's called self-preservation. It's the thing that makes you get out of bed for another day, even when you don't want to. I needed a change for Freya and me. I needed a chance of a new life for us both.'

He reached and brushed a thumb down her cheek.

She was so wise. He'd never met anyone like this before. There was so much more to learn about Bonnie Reid.

He'd shared with her tonight, and now she'd shared with him.

'Thank you,' he whispered.

Her pretty brow furrowed. 'For what?'

'For not leaving tonight.' It was the thing that had bothered him every step of the way back home. It was the thing that he'd dreaded. That he'd expected. Because that was what he deserved. And he knew that. But Bonnie Reid had just surpassed all of his expectations.

His heart squeezed. If he'd left this room as she'd decorated it, things would have been perfect. The fire flickering in the fireplace, the tree lights twinkling all around them. But he'd destroyed all that and brought them back to his white, harsh, empty walls.

Bonnie Reid deserved better than that. Freya Reid deserved better than that.

She licked her lips. It was the tiniest movement—a subconscious movement—but it was all that he needed. He moved forwards, not hesitating, his lips connecting with hers.

She tasted of strawberries mixed with wine. The remnants of her perfume drifted up his nose, the feel of her jumper connecting with the delicate skin at the bottom of his throat. She didn't seem to mind his wet jumper. She didn't seem to care that wine sloshed from his glass as he wrapped one arm around her and tangled the other hand through her hair.

That hair. He'd wanted to touch it from the moment he'd seen it. It was silky, falling through his fingers easily. But he didn't want it to fall through. He wanted to catch it—just as he wanted to catch her. So he wrapped it around his fingers, anchoring his hand at the back of her head as the kissing increased.

She pulled back—and for a horrible second he thought she was going to say this was all a terrible mistake. But she didn't. Bonnie Reid was taking charge.

She moved, lifting the glass from his hand and sitting it on the side table, then, pushing his shoulders back against the sofa, she swung one leg over him, so she was sitting on top of him.

She put her arms around his shoulders again and looked him straight in the eye. 'There. That's better.'

'It certainly is.' He didn't hesitate. He pulled her closer, feeling the warm curves of her breasts against his chest. He slid his hands up and under her jumper. Her smooth, silky skin beneath his fingertips. Everything about this felt right.

Her smell. Her taste. Her touch. Her fingers skirted around his neck and shoulders, along the line of his jaw, scratching against his stubble, then through his hair, pulling his lips hard against her own.

His tongue played around the edges of her mouth as their kiss deepened. Suddenly, these clothes were too much; they were stopping him from feeling exactly what he wanted to.

He drew back and pulled his wet jumper and shirt over his head, then pulled her soft jumper off, throwing it on the floor with his own.

Her round full breasts were encased in a cream lace bra. She was breathing heavily now, her body weight on the most sensitive part of him.

He ran his fingers across her shoulder, reaching the pale skin at the bottom of her neck and then down, over her breastbone, between her breasts and down to her navel, resting just above the button of her jeans.

She sucked in her stomach—an automatic reaction but an unnecessary one. He loved every part of her soft curves.

His brain was screaming 'no' to him right now. But his body just wasn't listening.

He shouldn't be doing this. Bonnie and Freya were in a vulnerable position right now. This was only a temporary arrangement. Jacob Layton didn't form attachments. Not like this.

But everything about this felt right. Everything about this had been simmering under the surface since his first meeting with Bonnie. Now it was exploding to the surface in volcanic proportions.

For his part, the attraction had just grown. The more he got to know her and Freya, the more he admired her. Her strength, her resilience, her determination to do a good job.

Her empathy with patients, her patience with staff. Her sense of humour, her stubborn streak and the way she answered back. Bonnie Reid was one of a kind.

And he was about to make the biggest mistake of his life.

Bonnie had already experienced one screwed-up partner. The last thing she needed was another. His hands stilled on her back.

Bonnie and Freya deserved a bright future. How could he give them one with his cancer history? That would always, permanently, hang over his head. He knew without asking that Bonnie would want more kids.

And he knew without thinking about it that he already believed the cancer was in his genes. He couldn't do that to a child. He couldn't do that to Bonnie and Freya.

'Jacob? Is everything okay?' She'd pulled back a little, a frown creasing her brow.

'Mummy?' The little voice cut through the emotions in the room.

Jacob froze. Bonnie did the opposite. She let out a little gasp, then flicked around, trying to locate her discarded jumper. She leapt off his lap and pulled the jumper over her head. Freya's voice hadn't sounded too close. She must be standing at the top of the stairs.

Jacob looked at his crumpled shirt and jumper, still together, but lying at Bonnie's feet. 'Do you want me to come?'

She shook her head quickly as she started towards the door. 'No, no, it's fine. Let me deal with Freya.'

His last view was of the bottom he so admired in those jeans. He heard her padding up the stairs in her bare feet. 'Hi, honey. What's wrong? Let's get you back to bed.' He heard the noise of her sweeping Freya into her arms and the voices faded quickly.

Jacob leaned forwards and put his head in his hands. What was he thinking? How could he have explained to Bonnie why he'd stopped kissing her, without telling her about his diagnosis—the one part of himself he still wanted to remain private?

His stomach twisted. He knew none of this was right. But Jacob didn't share. It didn't feel normal to him; it didn't feel natural. Telling Bonnie about his mother had been the first time in his life he'd ever really shared.

But the cancer diagnosis? No. He didn't want her to look at him that way. With pity. With sympathy. With the 'I'm sorry there's a chance you'll die' expression on her face.

He never wanted anyone to look at him like that—let alone Bonnie. He'd only told two colleagues—ones he trusted explicitly—and that was only because he'd had to reduce his patient contact while undergoing his most intense treatments. If he could have got away with telling no one that was exactly what he'd have done.

He sighed and leaned back against the sofa, his bare back coming into contact with the leather surface. It wasn't comfortable, not against bare skin. Somehow he hadn't noticed with Bonnie on his lap.

He looked around the room. White, stark walls.

It had looked so much better before.

He could admit that now. He could try and be rational about things. It seemed a little easier now he'd told Bonnie about his mother dying at Christmas.

He winced as he remembered the look of their faces earlier when he'd started to tear the decorations back down. How stupid. How pathetic. How ungrateful.

He stood up and grabbed his shirt and jumper from the floor, walking through to the kitchen and dumping them in the laundry basket. He had a pile of clothes sitting on top of the tumble dryer. He grabbed a T-shirt and walked back through to the hall.

He had to find a way to make things up to Bonnie and Freya. He hated that Freya might be scared of him now. He had to do something to change that.

He pulled open the hall cupboard door and was nearly speared in the face with Christmas tree branch. A single red bauble rolled past his feet. She'd stripped the Christmas tree but obviously kept all the decorations.

He gave a smile of relief. That was where she'd stored them.

He glanced at the empty banister. He might not have got some things right tonight, but if he wanted to make it up to them he knew exactly where to start.

CHAPTER EIGHT

BONNIE RUBBED HER sleep-ridden eyes. She'd had trouble sleeping after last night's events. Freya had only woken up to go to the toilet and been a little disorientated. Once Bonnie had cuddled her back into bed she'd fallen asleep instantly.

But Bonnie's head had been spinning. She'd been shocked by Jacob earlier. But she'd also known there had to be a reason behind it. A deep-seated reason. And that was why she'd given him the tiniest bit of leeway.

Now she understood. It didn't excuse his actions, but she knew exactly how sorry he was—it had been written over every inch of his face. And when he'd shared about his mother she couldn't help but cry.

Her thoughts immediately went to Freya. She couldn't stand the thought of something happening to her and Freya being left alone. Who would love her the way she did? Certainly not her father. Something prickled down her spine. If anything ever happened to her, Freya would automatically go to her father. What kind of life would she have with him? The kind of life that Jacob had endured as a child?

Her skin tingled as Jacob entered her thoughts. Who was she kidding? Had she just made the biggest mistake of her life?

Jacob had opened up to her. But there was still so much she didn't know about him—even though they were living under one roof. Maybe she was just being paranoid. But after living with an unfaithful, feckless husband, she wanted to go into any new relationship with her eyes wide open.

She'd been hurt. Freya had been hurt. She'd no intention of ever going down that road again. Self-preservation was a must. Even if any thought of him made her heart pitter-patter faster.

'Can we have breakfast, Mummy?' The little voice cut through her thoughts.

She turned and smiled at her little girl. She was blessed: Freya woke up each day in a good mood. She reached over and gave Bonnie a hug. 'I like it when you're in my bed, Mummy.'

She hugged back. 'I like it too. But it's only on special occasions. Now, what do you want for breakfast?'

'Toast and jam.'

'I think I can do that. Let's go to the toilet and wash our face and hands first.'

As they reached the top of the stairs she bent down to pick Freya up. It was just instinct—she'd done it most mornings since they'd got there. Freya wasn't used to stairs and Bonnie was always worried that she'd trip if she was still sleepy.

As she gathered Freya in her arms she realised something was a little off. It took her the first few steps to realise what it was. The red and green garland was wound back around the banister.

A smile started to edge around her lips. She kept walking. Now she could hear, and smell, activity in the kitchen. Someone was cooking bacon and singing while they cooked.

As she reached the bottom of the stairs the twinkling lights from the front room attracted her like a magnet. She walked back into the front room.

Everything was back exactly where it should be. 'Look, Freya,' she whispered.

The tree lights were twinkling, the branches redecorated with tinsel and baubles. The nativity scene was back on the side table. The red and green garland for the mantelpiece was back in place. She'd no idea how he'd managed to patch it together—but she didn't really care.

The fact was, he'd done it.

'Mummy, our tree's back up,' said Freya. A smile had lit up her face. 'Does Jacob like it now?'

Bonnie nodded slowly. 'I think he must.' She couldn't stop smiling. He'd revealed part of himself last night but now he'd obviously made the decision to try and move on.

The house felt full of warmth. It was so much nicer with the Christmas decorations up; it felt much more like a home, rather than just a house.

She carried Freya through to the kitchen. Jacob was putting a pot of tea on the kitchen table. 'Oh, you're up, good.' His eyes skirted over to Freya; he looked wary. 'I've made breakfast. Sit down.'

Freya stared at the plate of bacon as Bonnie put her in one of the chairs. 'I don't want bacon. I want toast and jam.'

Jacob smiled at her. 'I thought you might say that.' He produced a toast rack stacked full of toast and a jar of jam.

Bonnie smiled as she sat down. Freya reached over and grabbed a slice of toast. 'Can you butter this, Mummy?' Her eyes fixed on Jacob again. 'I like that the tree's back. I like the lights.'

A second of hesitation passed over Jacob's face before

he pulled out a chair and sat down next to Freya. 'I do too. I think it was a good idea to get a tree for the house. Thank you very much. I'm sorry if I seemed angry last night. I was just a little surprised.'

Bonnie held her breath as she handed over the buttered toast to Freya and opened the jar of jam. She wasn't entirely sure how Freya would respond.

But Freya just shrugged. 'Can we watch cartoons today?'

It was that simple for a five-year-old. No stomach churning. No fretting. She just accepted what he said and was happy that the tree was back up.

Jacob and Freya continued to chat over breakfast. Today, it seemed, was going to be a quiet day in the house.

Jacob seemed more at ease. Maybe he was just getting used to having people in his house—or maybe talking about his mother last night had helped him a little.

She certainly hoped so.

It was so strange to see Freya chatting away with him. Even when they'd lived with her husband, breakfast had usually been their time together. Robert had rarely appeared at the breakfast table. And last night's events seemed to have been quickly forgotten.

They laughed together and something twisted inside her. She wasn't quite sure what it was. Fear? Envy? Confusion?

Jacob seemed comfortable this morning—but was she? She'd kissed him last night. If Freya hadn't interrupted it might have become a whole lot more. Bonnie didn't usually act on impulse—not when it came to men. But things with Jacob last night had just seemed so natural. So heated.

It made her want to catch her breath.

This was a new job. A new city. A new life.

Just how much change was she ready for?

Jacob felt as if he'd been holding his breath since last night. Ever since he'd kissed Bonnie and realised exactly the effect she had on him.

Part of him was sorry. Now he would always know exactly what he was missing. Part of him wasn't the least bit sorry. It had been a long time since he'd felt a connection to someone. The fact that Bonnie was a mother hadn't even entered his head.

If you'd asked him a few years ago if he'd ever have a relationship with someone who had children he would have said an overwhelming no. But he'd have been wrong. With the exception of last night, he'd liked being around Freya. It was surprising him—just as much as it was probably surprising Bonnie and Freya.

He'd noticed the way people were looking at him at work. For the last ten days he'd felt differently. He'd felt lighter. This morning he practically felt so light he could float away. The only thing that was still anchoring him to the ground was his test results.

Even if—and he prayed they would be—they were good results, it still wouldn't change other things for Jacob. The cancer would always lurk in the background, always a possibility of a recurrence. Always that uncertainty of whether it was familial and he could pass it on. Gene mapping wasn't quite there yet to give him that answer.

But these last few days at home had felt so much better. Putting up the decorations again last night had given him a lot of thinking time. It was time to put the negative associations that he had with Christmas to bed.

His mother would have hated him being like this. Feeling like this about a season that should be the happiest of times.

The look on Freya and Bonnie's faces this morning when they realised he'd put the decorations back up had been enough for him. He was sure he'd done the right thing. He'd also done something else. He was still to find out if it was right or not.

He pushed some tickets along the table to Freya. 'I found out about a little surprise. I was wondering if you and your mum would like to come.'

Freya stared down at the tickets. The words were obviously too complicated for a five-year-old, but the pictures told a good story. She pointed. 'Is that Rudolph? Can we go and see Rudolph?'

Jacob looked up at Bonnie. He was feeling hopeful, even though he should probably have run this by her first. She leaned over and spun the tickets around. 'Today? The Christmas lights, a visit to Santa *and* a chance to meet the reindeers?' Surprise and amusement, with a tiny bit of disbelief, mixed through her voice as her eyebrows rose.

He nodded carefully. 'What do you think? Would you like to go?'

Her face relaxed and she lifted her mug of tea to take a sip. Her voice was quiet. 'I think that would be lovely. Thank you for thinking of us, Jacob.'

Her gaze met his. She was still thinking about last night.

He'd pulled back. She must be wondering why. Because the air between them still sizzled. It crackled. He still wanted to reach out and touch her cheek, kiss her lips. He just didn't want to be unfair.

He took a deep breath. 'I'll always think about you, Bonnie.'

Silence hung between them. It was probably the wrong

thing to say. It almost seemed as if he were finishing something that had never started. Truth was, he didn't have a clue what he was doing right now. But the implication was clear. Bonnie was affecting him. He *did* feel something for her—even if he didn't know what it was.

But those words seemed enough for Bonnie; she gave a little smile and stood up. 'Come on, Freya, the Christmas lights and Santa visit aren't until three o'clock this afternoon. Let's have a lazy morning on the sofa.'

Freya jumped up in agreement and ran out of the kitchen towards the front room, leaving Jacob at the kitchen table, eyes fixed on Bonnie's backside in her pyjama trousers, trying to keep his thoughts in check.

'Is everyone ready?'

They were all practically standing in a line. Winter jackets, scarfs, gloves and wellington boots in place. Freya couldn't stand still. She had ants in her pants. She didn't care that the temperature had plummeted again and a mixture of sleet and snow was starting to fall. She just wanted to meet Rudolph.

'Will I get to sit on his back? Will Donner be there? And Blitzen? Is his nose really red?'

The questions had been never-ending since this morning.

Jacob smiled. 'I have no idea. This is all new to me.'

Freya frowned. 'Is it far? Are we going in the car?'

Bonnie shook her head. 'No. We're going to walk. That way, we'll get to have plenty of time to see all the Christmas lights.'

'Will Fraser from school be going to see Santa too?'

Jacob knelt in front of her. 'And who might Fraser be?'

Freya tossed her red hair over her shoulder. 'My friend,' she said matter-of-factly.

Bonnie suppressed a laugh. 'Welcome to my world, Jacob. Or rather the world of little girls—a new best friend every day. I just try and keep up.'

Jacob folded his arms across his chest and did his best to look severe. 'Fraser, eh? Well, if he's there you'll need to point him out. I'd like to meet this Fraser.'

Freya giggled. 'Can I get my picture with Santa?'

Bonnie nodded and bent to straighten Freya's hat. 'Yes, it's all arranged. Now, are you ready?'

She jumped up and down. 'I've been ready for hours, Mum. Let's go!'

It was the perfect afternoon. Cold without being *too* cold. A light dusting of snow everywhere. By three o'clock it was already getting dark.

Freya's little hand was in Jacob's. It was surprising how comfortable it felt. How comfortable *he* felt doing this. Bonnie had a cream woollen hat pulled over her auburn hair and a thick green wool coat. She looked perfect. Like something from a Christmas card.

He swung Freya up into his arms. 'Come on. Let's go and visit Santa and the reindeers. It won't be long until the lights get switched on.'

The prepaid tickets were the godsend. Thank goodness for one of the midwives in the special care unit. She'd mentioned buying the tickets last year and not having to wait in the freezing cold for hours with her young kids.

Freya only had to wait five minutes before she was able to jump on Santa's knee and tell him what she wanted for Christmas. She counted off things on her finger. 'I'd like a new baby doll, one that can eat and poop. I like to change nappies,' she said proudly.

Santa nodded in amusement. 'I think that can be arranged,' he said, nodding towards Bonnie.

She was leaning against Jacob. 'Thank goodness it isn't Christmas Eve,' she said. 'Last year Freya announced she wanted some board game when we visited Santa on Christmas Eve. It was the first time she'd mentioned it at all. And, of course, it was after five o'clock on Christmas Eve.'

He wrapped his arm around her waist. It was so easy to do that. 'What did you do?'

She shook her head. 'What do you think I did? I panicked!'

He watched Freya. She was saying to Santa Claus, 'We really need a house too. We've just moved down from Scotland and we still haven't found somewhere else to stay.' She looked up into the air. 'I mean, the house we're staying in right now is perfect. So, if we could have one just like it, that would be great.'

'You like where you stay?' Santa asked.

Freya sighed. 'It's the most beautiful house in the world.'

Something twisted inside Jacob. He'd always loved his house—even if he hadn't really made his mark on it. But to hear someone else say those words out loud? Say that they loved his house—that was special. It almost made him feel warm inside.

And for the strangest reason, it didn't send him into a mad panic. He wanted Bonnie and Freya to feel welcome in his home. He liked having them around.

Bonnie shifted a little as if she were uncomfortable.

'But it could be more perfect.'

Jacob turned at the sound of Freya's voice. She had his full attention.

'What would make it perfect, then?' asked Santa.

'A dog,' Freya said quickly.

Jacob burst out laughing. 'She doesn't seem to be letting this one go, does she?'

Bonnie laughed too. 'I'll have to buy her a stuffed one for Christmas. Or maybe one of those ones that bark? There's no way we could deal with a real dog. Not with me working full-time. It just wouldn't be fair.'

Jacob nodded. 'You're right. I've always considered getting a dog, but even with all the dog-walking companies, it just didn't seem fair to leave a dog by itself all day.'

She looked surprised. 'You've thought about getting a dog?'

'Of course.' He winked. 'I've heard they're not as complicated as women, or...' he looked over at Freya '...five-year-olds!'

Bonnie laughed as Freya jumped down from Santa's lap and held out her hand towards him. 'Thanks, Santa, I'll let you know if I get what I asked for.'

Santa looked a little surprised and shot Bonnie and Jacob a smile as he shook Freya's outstretched hand. 'This is a very astute little girl. Merry Christmas to you all.'

They walked outside towards the reindeer pen and Bonnie pulled the bag of food they'd been given from her bag. One of the staff showed Freya how to hold the food in her hand and she screamed as a reindeer named Vixen slobbered all over her hand.

Without even thinking about it, Jacob stuck his hand in Bonnie's bag and pulled out the wipes that were sticking out, grabbing one out and wiping Freya's hand.

'Jacob?' He knelt down in front of her. 'Why don't the reindeers have red noses? Aren't they supposed to?'

He smiled. He loved the way Freya's mind worked. Her endless questions. Her five-year-old's logic. And her complete and utter belief in all things Christmas. This morning she'd shown him a website they'd been shown at school that would plot Santa's journey all the way around the world on Christmas Eve. They'd even been able to input the house address to let Santa know where they were.

He whispered in her ear. 'You've got to remember. It's not Christmas Eve yet. They don't fly until Christmas Eve, so they don't need their red noses until then.'

He could almost hear her thinking out loud. Finally she gave a little nod. 'Now I understand.'

His phone rang and he stood up and pulled it from his back pocket, looking to see who was calling. He glanced towards Bonnie and Freya and walked off to the side.

Bonnie looked up. It must be a work call. Jacob obviously didn't want to discuss a patient around them and that was fine.

Freya was still excited. In a few minutes' time it would be time for the countdown and switch-on of the Christmas lights. Bonnie held out her hand. 'Come on. The lights will be on in a few minutes. Let's find somewhere good to stand.'

The smells from the street vendors were wafting all around them. Roasting chestnuts, hot chocolate and mulled wine. The rich pine scents from the wreaths outside the nearby florist were mixing in with other aromas. Holly was intertwined amongst them and mistletoe hung from the door of the shop. Should she buy some?

Jacob was still talking. He looked worried; there were deep furrows across his brow. She crossed her fingers that there were no problems on the labour ward.

He caught her eye and turned away. Something twisted inside.

Now she was being stupid.

This was simple. This was just a nice day out between work colleagues—housemates. Because if she took that kiss out of the equation, there really wasn't anything else between them—was there?

In theory, no. But that wasn't the way she was feeling inside. And everything about that made her uncomfortable. After the nightmare of her ex-husband she'd vowed not to expose herself or Freya to anything like that again. She didn't need the hassle of the conflict.

Bonnie Reid fully intended to be a man-free zone. So what had gone wrong?

She hadn't even lasted a day. They'd moved in with Jacob their first day. How ridiculous was that?

From the initial grumpy meeting, Jacob had seemed to chill. She'd been nervous about staying there with Freya; the first few days she'd scoured the Internet for somewhere else.

But it was almost as if, after the first few days, he wasn't really in a hurry for them to move out. Anywhere she showed him he always had a reason for them not to move there. Too far out. Too rough. Not near a good school. And while it was helpful and informative, it wasn't actually inspiring her to move elsewhere.

She and Freya were getting a little too comfortable in Jacob's lovely house. It was almost starting to feel like home.

Jacob put the phone back in his pocket and spun around to face them. He walked over, picked up Freya and put her on his shoulders. 'This is where you'll get the best view,' he said, and she squealed with happiness as he swung her up.

But Bonnie's stomach was still churning. It was almost as if the phone call hadn't happened. It was almost as if he hadn't deliberately walked away from them and excluded them from his conversation.

A horrible chill crept down her spine. Jacob wasn't on call any more. His on-call duties finished at midday. Whoever had phoned him—it hadn't been about work. There were no patient confidentiality issues. So what didn't he want her to hear?

She didn't have time to think any further, because his arm was around her shoulders and he moved them forwards a little as Santa positioned himself on stage to make the announcement and turn on the lights.

Crowds had gathered all around them. They were lucky Jacob had thought to buy them tickets. The area in front of the stage was crushed full of people. At the side, they could see the view all along the street. A perfect position to see the lights switched on.

Santa started cheering the crowd on. Some of the handlers had brought the reindeers out from the pen and positioned them behind him. The animals seemed completely unperturbed by the noise or the crowds. Freya, in the meantime, was clapping her hands with excitement.

'Ten, nine, eight, seven, six.' Bonnie joined in the countdown with the rest of the crowd. This was what she wanted for her little girl. To be full of the joys of Christmas and to enter into the spirit of things.

Moving down here had been hard. Emotionally hard. The separation in miles was the final nail in her divorce coffin, and one that she so badly needed. Everything down here was new. Everything down here was fresh.

Living in a town where Freya could have seen her father at any point, and been ignored by him, was too much for her. His lack of involvement hurt. It wasn't the issue of being both mum and dad to her little girl—that was without question. It was the carefully chosen words she had to find to explain why he didn't call—why he didn't visit.

And it didn't matter that moving to Cambridge gave Robert a perfect excuse for not visiting Freya. He hadn't needed one in Scotland. It just lessened the impact of him not being around. Freya was so caught up in her new home, her new school and her new friends that she hadn't even had a chance to miss him and that was a welcome relief.

Jacob looked over at her and squeezed her shoulder. 'Okay?'

'Yes.' She nodded, pushing away all the other little doubts that had started to creep into her mind. It was one phone call. One. Nothing else.

Jacob wasn't Robert. And even if he was, it was none of her business. They were work colleagues—friends.

Santa finished the countdown, 'Three, two, one,' and flicked the switch.

It was magical. Like something from a movie. The Christmas lights started at the bottom of the street. Red, green and gold garlands strung across the road flickered to life.

It was like a Mexican wave. At points along the way there were bigger illuminations. A North Pole house, a multicoloured sleigh, a large pile of presents. The church halfway along the street had joined in. Multicoloured lights wrapped around the stained-glass windows and steeple lit up the dark night sky. A nativity scene in the churchyard, complete with shepherds and magi, was brought to life.

Freya loved every part of it. Every time another part lit she gasped with excitement. The lights were getting closer, finishing with the large Christmas tree in the middle of the square. The colours lit up one at a time, as if someone were stringing tinsel around the tree while they watched. First green, then red, then gold. Finally a large white twinkling star lit at the top of the tree as fireworks started to go off behind them. Cambridge really knew how to do Christmas.

One of the brass bands from the local schools started to play Christmas carols and Bonnie, Freya and Jacob joined in. By the time Jacob slid Freya off his shoulders an hour later her eyelids were heavy. Bonnie held out her arms to take her but Jacob shook his head. 'It's fine. We've still got quite a way to walk back.' She saw the tiniest flash of hesitation across his eyes, then he bent down and dropped a kiss on her lips.

Just when she thought she had things sorted in her head. Just when she'd convinced herself that what Jacob did was none of her business and she should forget their last kiss.

The kiss zapped everything back into his place. The taste of his lips and the feel of his hands sliding under her jumper and up her back.

'Come on.' He smiled at her. 'Let's get sleepyhead back home. It's getting cold out here.'

A few gentle flakes of snow started to fall around them. Freya had automatically snuggled into Jacob's neck and was already half asleep. Jacob kept his other arm around Bonnie and steered them both through the crowd and along the street.

Bonnie looked around. To everyone else, they must look like a regular family. Mum, Dad and little girl. Part of that terrified her. The other part pined for it.

She wanted Freya to be loved, to be part of a family. She wanted her little girl to have the relationship that she'd missed out on with her own father.

And Bonnie didn't want to grow old alone. She'd been

stung by her cheating ex and it had made her wary. But it didn't stop her hoping that somewhere out there would be a man who would love and respect her the way she did him.

Would make her skin tingle and send pulses through her body from a mere look, a touch.

Trouble was, the only person who fitted the bill right now was Jacob Layton.

Could she really trust him with her heart? And with Freya's too?

CHAPTER NINE

JACOB STARED AT the letter in his hand.

This was it. The appointment he'd been waiting for. The one that could be the end of the big black cloud that had been hanging over his head for the last fifteen months.

His scheduled appointment was fourteen days away but he'd phoned and asked for a cancellation. He couldn't wait any longer to find out his results—good or bad.

Professional courtesy in the NHS went a long way. CT scan and blood tests tomorrow. Appointment with the specialist the day after.

His stomach twisted. Over the last few days he'd reverted to form and he knew it. He was snapping at people again, being grumpy at work.

All because of what was happening inside.

Something had hit him. Ever since he'd had that conversation with Bonnie and kissed her he couldn't think straight. His house was now full of Christmas decorations and happy, smiley people. And for the first time in his life he actually wanted to be a happy, smiley person too.

But he just couldn't be. Not with this hanging over his head.

The possibility of a real relationship—a real connection with someone—was there. But he felt as if it were slipping through his fingers like shifting sands.

Talking about his mother had been an enormous help. Sharing with Bonnie had given him a connection he hadn't felt since he was a young child. Bonnie was a woman he could trust. A woman he could love with his whole heart.

His grip tightened on the letter in his hand. So why hadn't he told her about this?

The truth was he wasn't ready. Cancer was a burden. Cancer was a relationship deal breaker. He was still at that uncertain stage with Bonnie. He didn't want to be a burden to her and Freya—particularly if the news he was about to receive was bad.

If it was, he would step back and fade into the background of their lives. He would probably stop making up reasons she shouldn't move to any of the properties that she'd shown him and help her and Freya take the next steps in their lives.

Above everything he didn't want Bonnie to feel sorry for him. To form a relationship with him out of sympathy or pity. He didn't want that kind of relationship.

He wanted the kind that had started to burn inside him already. The kind where she was his first thought in the morning and his last thought at night. The kind where he could walk into the labour suite and sense she was there without even seeing her.

The kind where her scent would drift across the room towards him and wrap itself around him like a magic spell. So the first face he would see would be hers and her smile would send him a thousand unspoken promises.

Bonnie and Freya had been badly let down before. He didn't want that for them again. And until he found out about his test results, he couldn't even begin to have the kind of conversations with Bonnie that he should be having.

Would she even consider their relationship progressing? How would she feel knowing that he'd had cancer? How would she feel about his position on children? She already had Freya, but Bonnie struck him as the kind of woman who'd want to expand her family. Could she be in a relationship with a man who didn't want to pass the risk of cancer—no matter how small—on to his kids?

So many unanswered questions. So many dangerous assumptions. Crabbit. That was how she'd good-naturedly described him the other day. It was a good Scottish word for him—because that was exactly how he felt.

Unsure. That was another word that described him right now.

He'd always spent his life knowing exactly who he was and what he wanted.

Bonnie—and Freya—had literally turned his world upside down.

'Jacob?'

He crumpled the paper in his hand and thrust it into his pocket. 'Yes?' Bonnie was standing at his office door. A furrow ran across her brow.

'Sean just phoned. Someone else phoned in sick for tomorrow. He wondered if you could cover the theatre list?'

Jacob hesitated. He'd never refused to cover for a fellow doctor before. His automatic default position was always to say yes.

But this was different. If he missed the tests tomorrow, he'd have to wait another two weeks before his routine appointment came up. There were another four obstetricians at CRMU. Sean had probably just asked him first as a matter of routine. He took a deep breath. 'No. Sorry, tell him I have obligations that I can't break. He'll need to ask someone else.'

Bonnie hesitated and took a little step towards him. 'Jacob?'

He shook his head. He couldn't have this conversation with her—not right now. He swept past her, before her light perfume started to invade his senses. 'Tell him to ask Isabel. I'm sure she'll oblige.'

He carried on down the corridor. One look from Bonnie's confused blue eyes was enough for him. He had to be so careful. She'd been hurt badly by her husband. He'd already done damage when he'd torn down the Christmas decorations. For the next two days it would be best if he could avoid her. He'd find a reason to work late tonight. And another reason to stay out of her way tomorrow. His tests were in the afternoon. Then he'd just have to wait twenty-four hours to find out his results.

He glanced at his watch. He needed to have a conversation with Dean Edwards about a baby in Special Care. He could go there. Bonnie would be tied up in the labour suite for the rest of the day.

He sucked in a breath as he pushed open the swing doors. Forty-eight hours. Forty-eight hours, then he'd know if his life was about to begin, or could be about to end.

CHAPTER TEN

SOMETHING WAS WRONG. She could feel it in her bones.

Jacob was avoiding her—and avoiding Freya. Last night he'd come home when they'd both been in bed. When she'd got up and gone downstairs to make a cup of tea and talk to him, it had been obvious he had other things on his mind.

It was painful. It was embarrassing to be around someone that had kissed her so passionately a few days before and now acted as though he didn't want her around.

Maybe it stung so much because she actually cared. She cared what Jacob thought about her.

And caring was the one thing she shouldn't be doing.

Jacob had told her about his mother. But there was something else he was keeping from her. And it made her uncomfortable.

She deserved better than that—Freya deserved better than that.

Worse than anything, she didn't even feel as if she could call him on it. They weren't even in a proper relationship. She had no right to ask where he was going, or what he was doing. She just had that horrible sensation of being taken for a fool.

It didn't help that she was staying in his house. In fact, it made things ten times worse. If she'd met him through work and they'd maybe just shared a kiss, or gone on a date, she would be able to take a step back and distance herself.

Living under one roof made things a whole lot more complicated.

She tapped at the computer screen. It was only a few weeks until Christmas and the choices seemed even more limited than the last time she'd looked. Seven flats—all within her price range. All white, bland, soulless rooms in a range of buildings she wasn't sure she wanted to stay in.

Two in tower blocks. Three in areas that were less than salubrious. And that hadn't come from Jacob—a few of the other members of staff in the labour suite had recounted tales of staying in some of the surrounding areas. One looked in the same state as the motel she and Freya had stayed in, and another was nearer Freya's school but was a tiny one-bedroom flat.

She clicked on another that flashed by on the top of her screen. This time it was a beautiful two-bedroom flat well out of her price range. A large, spacious flat with original polished floorboards like Jacob's and the same bay-style windows dressed with the kind of curtains she'd imagined for his house.

She pressed the delete button quickly. She was being stupid. Even her house search reminded her of him.

She scribbled down the details of the tiny one-bedroom flat. She'd phone the agent later. How much space did she really need anyway? As long as the place was heated and didn't suffer from damp it would be fine. It had the essential ingredients. It was near Freya's school and it would be a place to call their own.

A tiny shiver crept down her spine. It had always been her intention to find somewhere for her and Freya to stay. She'd allowed herself to be distracted by Jacob.

She'd let herself be influenced by him when he'd told her everything she'd looked at was unsuitable. In a few short weeks, she and Freya had become comfortable in his home.

The sharp man she'd met on her first day had all but vanished. Once you scratched beneath the surface with Jacob Layton there was so much more. He was just good at hiding all the stuff that was really important. His sense of humour, his warmth, his vulnerability and his strength.

'Bonnie? Can you come and give us a hand? We've just been phoned. We've got a woman who is thirty-two weeks pregnant with twins coming in by ambulance. They think the babies are in distress.' Karen, one of the junior midwives, was at the door.

Bonnie clicked the window on the computer to close it and stood up quickly. 'No problem, Karen.' She walked out of the office and across to the treatment room to wash her hands and put on an apron. 'Which room are you preparing?'

Karen glanced over at the whiteboard. 'Room 3, I think. That's the biggest. I'll go and page the on-call obstetrician.'

Bonnie felt her stomach flip over. One of the obstetricians was off sick. There was every chance Jacob would now be on call.

She finished the final checks in the room just as the ambulance crew wheeled the patient in. 'Hi, Bonnie. This is Eleanor Brooks. She's thirty-two weeks pregnant with twins. Hasn't felt well the last few days and fainted in the street around thirty minutes ago.'

Bonnie moved over to the side of the bed and grabbed the edge of the sheet as the paramedic pulled Eleanor over on the patient slide board.

'Hi, Eleanor, I'm Bonnie, the sister in the labour suite.

Let me help you off with your jacket and we'll see how you're doing.'

Eleanor gave a nod and shrugged her shoulders out of her jacket, letting Bonnie pull it away as she lay back against the pillows. Her colour was poor and it only took Bonnie a few seconds to wind the blood-pressure cuff around her arm and start to inflate it.

Karen appeared again with the paperwork and spoke in a low voice for a few minutes with the ambulance crew.

'Eleanor, is there someone I can phone for you?'

Eleanor nodded towards her bag. 'My mobile is in there. My husband is John, but he works offshore on the rigs. You might not be able to get him. My mum's number is in there too. She lives in Cambridge.'

Karen glanced in Bonnie's direction; Bonnie gave her a silent nod. 'Is your husband up in Aberdeen?' She was calculating in her head how long it would take to helicopter him back from the rigs to the mainland, and then down to Cambridge. She blinked at the reading on the screen from the BP cuff. Karen's eyes widened.

'Have you seen your community midwife lately, Eleanor?'

Eleanor's blood pressure was unusually high. Any woman with a twin pregnancy was normally monitored quite closely. Eleanor shook her head. 'I had an appointment last week but she was off sick, and this week I wasn't feeling well enough to go, so I missed it.'

Karen scribbled a little note on the paperwork. 'I'll go and make these calls, chase up the obstetrician and arrange for Eleanor's notes.'

Bonnie gave a nod. 'Eleanor, can you tell me how you've been feeling this past week?'

'Awful.' The one-word answer said everything.

'Did you call your midwife for some advice?'

Eleanor sighed. Her eyes were half closed; it was obvious she was tired. Her legs and ankles were puffy. Bonnie bent over and gave the skin a gentle squeeze between her fingers, the imprint of her fingers clearly denting the skin.

'I didn't want to bother my midwife. I thought I'd feel better in a day or so. Everyone's had a viral thing lately. I was sure I had the same.'

Eleanor moved uncomfortably, ignoring Bonnie at her ankles and taking a little gasp of breath as she pressed her hand against her right-hand ribs.

'Eleanor? Are you having pain?'

Eleanor grimaced and nodded. The pain was too high up to be a labour pain, but it could indicate something else. The pain seemed to pass quickly and she relaxed a little. 'I've been tired. Really tired. But that's normal for twin pregnancies, isn't it? I've been feeling a bit sick too. I've had a headache for the last few days. I actually vomited twice yesterday—I've never done that before. And usually I'm peeing all the time, now I'm hardly peeing at all.'

Alarm bells were going off in Bonnie's head. Eleanor was showing some signs of pre-eclampsia. It wasn't that unusual in twin pregnancies, but Eleanor's condition seemed to be taking a dangerous turn.

She put her hand on Eleanor's arm. 'I know I've just got you into bed. But do you think you could manage to give me a urine sample? I know you said you're hardly peeing right now, but if you could squeeze something out that would be great.' She hesitated for a second. 'I'm also going to call the phlebotomist to take some bloods.'

Eleanor gave a little sigh and swung her legs around while Bonnie brought a commode into room. Right now, she didn't even want Eleanor walking into the separate bathroom. She wanted to monitor her at all times.

Karen came back into the room as Bonnie was helping Eleanor back into bed. She pressed the button on the blood-pressure monitor again. Karen held up some foetal monitors. 'I thought you might want me to attach these? And Sean is outside.'

Bonnie nodded as she wheeled the commode towards the door. 'Will you stay here until I get back?' Karen gave the tiniest nod of her head. They were both aware of the seriousness of the situation.

It only took Bonnie two minutes to dipstick the small sample of urine and put the rest in a collection bottle for the lab.

Once she'd washed her hands she went back outside. But Sean wasn't alone. He'd been joined at the desk by Jacob.

Her stomach flipped over. This was work. He couldn't avoid her—no matter how much he tried to.

Sean turned to face her. 'Can you give me an update?'

Bonnie nodded. Aware that Jacob still wasn't really looking at her.

'Eleanor Brooks is thirty-four. She's thirty-two weeks pregnant with twins. I've not seen her notes, but I'm assuming her pregnancy has been unremarkable up until now. She collapsed in the street earlier today. She has upper-right-quadrant pain, pitting oedema in her ankles, her blood pressure is one-sixty over one-ten. Pulse eighty-seven. I've just tested her urine and it's positive for protein.'

She watched as Sean scribbled some notes. 'There's more. She's had a headache the last few days, vomited twice yesterday and she's been very tired.'

Jacob frowned. 'Hasn't she seen a midwife at any point?'

Bonnie felt automatically defensive. 'She should have. She was last seen three weeks ago. The week after that, her midwife was sick, and last week she felt too unwell to attend. She didn't call in to speak to the midwife as she thought she just had a virus.'

Jacob started to swear under his breath. 'This is looking like HELLP syndrome. Do you mind if I come with you, Sean? We might need to do an emergency twin delivery.'

'Glad of the help,' Sean said quickly. He handed some blood forms to Bonnie. 'Can you get these done as an emergency?'

'No problem.' She took them as Sean and Jacob walked into the room to assess Eleanor. Five minutes later the ward clerk arrived with the notes and the phlebotomist answered her page. Bonnie flicked through the notes. Nothing untoward. All Eleanor's previous appointments had shown a healthy developing pregnancy.

The missed appointments were unfortunate. She just wished Eleanor had phoned her midwife when she'd started to feel unwell. Maybe her condition could have been picked up sooner. HELLP was serious. It could be life-threatening for both mother and babies.

Symptoms could be vague but it always started with pre-eclampsia. One of the crucial tests was the blood work and the quickest turnaround time from the lab would be just over an hour. Eleanor was already showing some of the classic signs.

Sean and Jacob came out of the room, both talking in low voices. The phlebotomist arrived, picked up the blood forms and went to collect the samples that would be needed.

'I think we should prepare and contact the anaesthetist anyway. Give her an ace-inhibitor to try and bring her blood pressure down and don't leave her alone.' Those last words were aimed at Bonnie. It was the first time his eyes had connected with hers.

There was something wrong—which was stupid, because she knew that already. But the look in Jacob's eyes? It was almost blank. As if there had never been anything between them, and there never would be.

Focus. She sucked in her breath. There was a patient to deal with. But as soon as Eleanor's condition was under control, Bonnie was definitely calling the letting agency.

She'd become too attached to him. *They'd* become too attached to him, too quickly. It was time to take stock. To take a breath.

She'd made a massive mistake with Robert. She'd married a man she didn't really love. When it came to men— her previous choice hadn't been great. Could she really trust her own judgement now?

Her heart was telling her one thing and her head another. It was all too much.

The phlebotomist appeared and waved the blood bottles at them. 'I'll take these direct to the lab and ask for the results to be phoned direct.'

Sean gave a nod. 'Thanks.' He turned to face Jacob. 'If I speak to the anaesthetist now are you free to assist in Theatre if required?'

There was silence for a few seconds. The quiet made Bonnie look up. Jacob always responded immediately. He never hesitated over clinical care.

But this time he did. This time he glanced at his watch. She could see him swallow as if a million things were flashing through his brain. 'I'll need to make a call to try to delay something else.'

Sean looked just as surprised as Bonnie. 'No problem. I can always find Isabel. She's covering the other theatre list today—but we can cancel the routine procedures for an emergency.'

That was right. The other theatre list. The one that Jacob had refused to cover today because he had somewhere else to be. Where exactly was that?

A whole wash of memories flooded over her. Robert. Continually making excuses about where he was going or where he had been. The way he could never look her in the eye when he'd been telling her those lies. Her stomach was in knots. She hated that Jacob was following the same pattern. He could never know how much those memories and associations hurt.

Jacob wasn't Robert. He would never be Robert. But he was definitely hiding something. It made her question herself. It made her question her judgement. Her choices had been wrong before. It felt as if she could be walking down the same path.

Where on earth was he going? And why was he being so evasive about it?

Jacob waved his hand at Sean. 'It will be fine. Give me five minutes to make the call. Let's just try and make sure that if we need to take Eleanor to Theatre there are no delays and we're ready to go as soon as we get the blood results.'

Sean nodded towards Bonnie. His initial surprise had died away and now he just looked relieved that he didn't have to go and call Isabel. What was the deal with those two?

'I'm going to stay close by. Give me a shout if you need anything.'

Bonnie went back to the room to help Karen. It only took a few minutes to administer the blood-pressure

drugs and start some IV fluids. Karen continued to monitor the babies and Bonnie set the blood-pressure cuff for
every ten minutes.

Eleanor kept her eyes closed, occasionally wincing
and touching her right side. It was a clear sign that her
liver was affected.

Jacob seemed impatient. He was pacing up and down
the corridor, and phoned the lab twice to harass them for
the blood results. She'd never seen him quite so on edge.

On one hand, she knew that he was putting the care of
Eleanor and her babies first. On the other, it was obvious
he was anxious to still keep his other plans.

The anaesthetist, Laura, appeared and did a quick
assessment. While Eleanor's current condition was
serious she had no significant history that would cause
any Theatre delays.

Laura was already dressed in theatre scrubs and
tucked her hair into her hat as the phone rang. Jacob
snatched it up, listening carefully before putting it back
down. 'Her blood tests confirm thrombocytopenia and
liver dysfunction.' These, combined with her other symptoms, meant that Eleanor could be at risk of liver rupture,
uncontrolled bleeding or cerebral oedema.

'Let's go, then,' said Laura. 'I'll meet you in Theatre
once you've spoken to Eleanor.'

Things moved quickly. Eleanor's mother arrived with
news that her husband was already on the helicopter and
had left the oil rig. It would still be hours before he arrived.

Eleanor's condition was worsening. She was beginning to get drowsy, so once Jacob had explained what
was happening and consented her they prepared her for
Theatre in a matter of minutes and whisked her down
the corridor.

Jacob and Sean disappeared to scrub and Bonnie hurried back to the labour ward.

It was three long hours before she heard anything else.

Sean walked up to the nursing station and pulled his theatre hat off his head. His mussed-up hair and tired eyes said everything. She looked over his shoulder. 'Where's Jacob?'

Sean shrugged. 'As soon as we had stabilised Eleanor and the babies and everyone was happy he disappeared.'

She bit her lip to stop her saying what she actually thought. 'What about Eleanor and her babies?'

Sean nodded. 'Two girls. Both in SCBU. Three pounds, four ounces and three pounds, two ounces. Not bad for twins. One had to have a little support breathing and the other was fine.'

'And Eleanor?'

He sighed. 'She started bleeding out almost straight away. Her blood pressure plummeted and she had six units of blood and then some platelets. We caught her just in time.'

'What's happening now?'

'She's stable. Mainly thanks to Jacob. She's been transferred to ICU. They need to keep a careful watch for organ failure.'

Bonnie sighed. 'Poor woman. I hope she's going to be okay. Will you let me know how she is?'

Sean raised his eyebrow. 'Won't Jacob tell you?'

Bonnie felt colour rush into her cheeks. 'What do you mean?'

Sean seemed completely unperturbed. He leaned on the desk towards her, a cheeky grin on his face. 'You two had a fight? For a few weeks the world of CRMU thought you'd turned Jacob into Prince Charming. But now he's back to his usual lovely self. I take it Prince Charming has turned into a frog?'

Sean was good-natured. He was only teasing but she felt distinctly uncomfortable. She wagged her finger at him. 'If I find out you've been gossiping about me, Sean, I'll ban you from our tea room. Don't think I don't know who goes in there and eats all the biscuits and sweets.'

Sean pulled back in mock horror. 'Ouch. Tough sanctions.' He waved his hand as he started down the corridor. 'Don't worry, Bonnie. All your secrets are safe with me.'

She blushed again as one of the other midwives came out of a patient's room and raised her eyebrows at the comment. She pulled her phone from her pocket. Enough was enough. It was time to make that call to the letting agency.

'Mummy, where are we going?' Freya was looking at the photo on the laptop screen.

Bonnie took a deep breath. 'We're going to stay somewhere else, honey. This was only ever temporary. Jacob let us stay for a few weeks until we could find somewhere for ourselves.'

'But I like it here. I like staying with Jacob.' Freya stuck her chin out and folded her arms across her chest.

I like staying with Jacob too.

She knelt down in front of Freya. 'I know that, honey. But we have to find a home of our own.' She tucked Freya's hair behind her ear and turned the computer screen around to show her the flat she'd just reserved. 'It will be fine. Honestly, it's near to the school and you'll still get to see all your friends.'

Freya gave a nod and stared at the cases. 'Will we have a Christmas tree like Jacob's?'

No. Something tugged at her heartstrings. She didn't want to leave. She *really* didn't want to leave.

Jacob was being secretive. He'd kissed her, but never made any promises. He'd never even asked her and Freya to stay for Christmas. He hadn't asked them to leave either…in fact, he'd made lots of excuses for them not to leave. But it wasn't the same.

A distant, secretive man was not what she needed. No matter how much he made her heart flip over. It made her question herself all the time. She needed to protect her heart and her daughter's. They'd got too attached. Freya's reaction now just made her even more determined.

Tears were bristling in her eyes. 'We'll get another Christmas tree and I promise it will be just as gorgeous as the one we decorated here.' *Bang goes my limited budget.*

It was fine. She would make sure it was fine. Anything to keep Freya settled after all the disruption she'd exposed her to. She already had the ridiculously expensive doll and all her accessories that Freya wanted for Christmas. Blowing what little savings she had left on another set of Christmas decorations was an easy sacrifice.

The key turned in the lock and she heard footsteps coming towards the sitting room. Jacob. He opened the door and his face dropped as soon as he saw what they were doing. The flat was clearly visible on the laptop screen in front of them.

'Bonnie? Freya? What's going on?'

Bonnie could feel her heart beating against her chest. She hadn't expected Jacob to come home—not when he'd been avoiding them. She'd planned to write him a note, thanking him for his hospitality, but saying they'd found somewhere to stay and she'd see him at work.

She put her arm around Freya's shoulders. 'Oh, Jacob, I didn't expect to see you. It's just—' she held out her hand '—I think we might have outstayed our welcome. I've found somewhere for us to stay.' She met his confused gaze. 'I think it's time for Freya and I to move on.'

His mouth was slightly agape. He looked shocked. He looked a bit hurt. And everything about this was confusing her.

This was definitely the right thing to do. This was *absolutely* the right thing to do.

'I'll miss you, Jacob.' Freya's little voice cut through the silence. 'Thank you for letting us stay.'

Jacob knelt down opposite her. 'I'll miss you too, Freya.' His voice sounded hoarse. 'You...and your mother.' He didn't look up. He didn't look at Bonnie at all.

This was it. This was his chance to say something. To tell Bonnie that his feelings were every bit as strong as hers.

That he wanted to kiss her again—just as he had the other night.

That he wanted to spend more time with her and Freya. That he wanted to give this relationship a chance. That this actually *was* a relationship.

That she wasn't completely crazy, and he was as crazy about her as she was about him.

She held her breath. Waiting. Waiting. For something. For anything.

But nothing came. Jacob still couldn't look her in the eye.

'Freya, go and get your coat and shoes. We need to go to the shops.' Freya disappeared without a word.

He lifted his head. 'Why are you leaving? Why are you leaving *now*?'

It was the way he said the word. She stepped forwards, everything erupting to the surface. 'We can't be here any more. Freya's getting too used to being around you.' She lifted her eyes. 'And so am I.'

She gave her head a shake. 'This was a bad idea. You helped us out, thank you. But I have no idea what's happening between us, Jacob.' She held out her hands. 'I have no idea what *this* is.' She took a deep breath. 'I've found somewhere for us to go. We'll be out of your hair.'

'You have? Where? Is it one of those ones that you showed me?' He sounded automatically defensive—as if he were going to tell them not to go.

She shook her head. 'No, it's another. It's small, but in the area of Freya's school. It will suit us for the next few months until we can find something else.' She licked her lips. This was horrible. This was awkward.

There was a huge hand currently inside her chest, squeezing her heart hard.

Jacob looked at her again. There was a flash of something behind his eyes, which disappeared almost instantly. He looked down again.

'What's going on, Jacob? I know something's been bothering you the last few days. But you haven't said anything. You've been avoiding me. I thought we could talk about things.' Her voice was edged with hopefulness that he might actually respond.

He shook his head. 'There's nothing.' His voice was flat.

His dismissal made her mad. 'Don't say that. Don't say it's nothing. I know it is. Tell me. Tell me what's going on.' She was shouting now and she could almost see all his barriers being built up all around him. She bit her lip in anger and tried one last time. 'I thought we could share things. I told you about my past—and you told me about yours. At least I thought you had.'

She glanced towards the door, worried that Freya would reappear.

He sucked in a deep breath. It made him seem taller,

his chest wider and more imposing. 'Not everything can be shared. Not everything is your business.' His words were clipped.

'Then we have to go,' she said quietly. 'I can't be around you, Jacob. I can't watch my little girl forming a closer attachment to you day by day when I feel as if you can't be honest with me.' She picked up her green coat. 'I've been down this road before.' Her eyes swept down to the floor and she gave a little shake of her head. 'I thought that this time I could trust my judgement.' She lifted her head and met his gaze. 'I guess I was wrong.'

There was silence for a few seconds.

'I hope you'll be happy,' he said quietly.

Something inside her died. That was it. Nothing else.

She'd been wrong. She'd been wrong about her and Jacob. There was nothing between them. A wave of humiliation washed over her.

She'd never felt like such a fool—not even when she'd found Robert in bed with her friend. Everything about this was different. With Robert, there had been no emotional investment left. With Jacob?

This hurt. This hurt so much it felt as if it could kill her.

Freya appeared at the door and she took her hand. 'Goodbye, Jacob.' Her voice was trembling. She just hoped he didn't notice.

She held herself straight and lifted her head before she opened the door and walked outside.

It was definitely time to go.

CHAPTER ELEVEN

JACOB TUGGED AT the collar of his shirt. It had never seemed tight before, but today it was cutting into him.

He hadn't slept a wink last night. Probably because everything about yesterday felt wrong and his house was...empty.

He shuffled on the seat and glanced at his watch for the hundredth time. He wasn't good at being a patient. Probably because he wasn't exactly that—patient. He watched as the door to the consultant's office opened and he sat up anxiously. The woman sitting next to him rustled her newspaper nervously as she was called in. He sighed and leaned back again.

That woman looked exactly the way he did—sick with worry. It was so strange being on the other side of the fence. This was exactly why he'd gone into obstetrics. He wanted to help life into the world. He wanted people to have joy in their lives.

Oncology services? Never. He hated having to give any expectant mother bad news. Imagine having to do this almost every day? He couldn't stomach that.

Right now he couldn't think about all the cancer success stories.

His insides clenched once again as he took some deep breaths. Worst-case scenarios. That was all that was running through his head right now. Stepping back from colleagues, stepping back from the job that he loved so he could undergo another set of treatment. Feeling sick to his stomach for days on end. Forgetting completely about any chance of a relationship with Bonnie and Freya. Living the rest of his life alone.

It wasn't what he wanted. *None* of this was what he wanted.

But the way he felt right now? There was no way he could put this on Bonnie and Freya.

What he wanted was a fiery redhead and her adorable daughter.

The words he'd wanted to say yesterday had stuck in his throat. *Don't go. Stay with me, please—even though I'm not sure I can offer you a future.* He couldn't put himself out there—not until he really knew what he was offering.

But one thing she'd said had affected him more than others. Freya was becoming too attached. He felt it too. And it seemed entirely natural. As if that was the way it should be. Because the little part of his heart he hadn't blocked off *wanted* to feel like that. But right now, his brain couldn't even let himself go there.

He was finding it hard enough to deal with himself without having to worry about other people's feelings. He couldn't even begin to imagine forming a relationship with Freya, only for her to have to be told down the line that her parent figure had died.

He knew exactly what that did to a kid. He could never wish that on another.

His house had been hideously empty last night. It was odd; it had never felt that way before. When he'd lived alone he'd never noticed the silence.

But last night he had. Every noise had seemed to echo

through the empty rooms. Taking out one cup for coffee, or one glass for wine, had seemed pathetic. Finding Freya's plastic cup in the sink had made his hands shake and for a second he'd thought he might break down.

The pain he'd felt last night was familiar.

Bonnie had left. His mother had left. Not in the same way, of course. But he felt every bit as raw now as he had all those years ago.

The pressure of the waiting game was almost breaking him.

The hands on his watch moved oh-so-slowly. Ten minutes felt like two hours. He just wanted to know. Even if the test results were bad at least he could start making plans.

He jumped as the door opened and the woman came back out, a stunned expression on her pale face. Did she get good news, or bad?

'Jacob Layton?'

He was on his feet in an instant.

'Come in, please.'

For a second his feet were stuck to the floor, but he was too determined to get this part over with to let anything hold him back. He took long strides into the room, not waiting to be offered a seat, his eyes scanning the notes upside down on the desk. Trying to see if they would reveal anything.

The oncology consultant closed the door and took his seat opposite Jacob. Desmond Carter had looked after Jacob throughout his treatment. As soon as he'd been diagnosed, Jacob had looked for the best. Someone who would understand his need to continue to work and be able to tailor his treatment to his needs.

Desmond should probably have retired years ago. His

hair was grey, his face deeply lined. But it appeared he loved his job as much as Jacob loved his.

He gave Jacob a little nod of acknowledgement. Another thing Jacob liked about Desmond Carter—he was a straight talker. He didn't give false platitudes and he told it like it was.

He glanced down at the notes in front of him. 'Jacob, let's talk about these test results.'

Bonnie was on edge. She was nervous about having moved to the new tiny flat just before Christmas. Nervous about the impact on Freya. Nervous about how she felt now she was out from under Jacob's roof.

It's temporary. She kept repeating the words in her head—hoping she might start to believe them.

She'd had to do it. Had to. She couldn't go on like this. Her insides had been so screwed up last night, praying, just praying Jacob might say something to her about how he felt. When it hadn't happened she'd spent the rest of the night crying into her pillow. Pathetic.

This was about her. This wasn't really about Jacob.

She was scared. Scared of putting herself out there and getting into a relationship with another man. She'd vowed to herself that if she ever got involved again, she would be absolutely sure. There wouldn't be a hint of doubt in her head.

But if Jacob couldn't tell her how he felt about her and Freya…then she was right. She was right to move out and give herself some headspace. Some time to make sure she could trust her judgement when it came to men.

The labour suite was busy today. All the staff kept joking about a power cut in Cambridge nine months before. And it certainly felt like that—she'd been catching babies all day.

But she hadn't caught sight of Jacob all day. It was probably just as well. He was bound to be avoiding her again. The further she pushed Jacob Layton from her mind, the better.

She finished stripping a bed in one of the rooms and walked along the corridor to the sluice. It was all hands on deck today; they even had a few midwives from some of the other areas helping out.

As she walked past the treatment room she glimpsed Isabel in a conversation with Hope.

Both had always been warm and friendly towards her—even inviting her to join them for dinner—and Jacob had mentioned that he was friends with both women. It struck her as a little strange. He seemed to hold them both in high regard, but she hadn't really seen him talking with either one.

'What's going on with Jacob?' Bonnie's footsteps stilled as Isabel's Australian accent floated out towards her.

They were drawing up a controlled drug for a pregnant woman in labour.

'How would I know?' answered Hope. 'I can barely get him to talk to me these days. It's a shame, but for a while we started to see the old Jacob again.'

Bonnie walked into the sluice and pushed the laundry into one of the baskets. She wasn't trying to overhear, but the two rooms were right next to each other with only a thin corridor leading to the sister's office separating them. She could still hear every word. She walked over to the sink to wash her hands.

'Do you think it's the cancer again?'

She froze. *What?*

Hope sounded serious. 'Do you think it's back? Oh, no. Don't say that. Not after everything he's been through.'

'Wouldn't he be due to get reassessed again? Some tests to see if the treatment's worked?'

The water was trickling in front of her but she hadn't moved.

Jacob. Jacob had cancer. *Her* Jacob had cancer and hadn't told her.

No. He couldn't possibly have. This couldn't be right. She held out her hands automatically, going through the motions of washing and drying them.

He hadn't lost his hair. It was short. But not missing. She hadn't noticed any marks on his skin for IV chemotherapy. He hadn't been sick around her. He didn't look sickly.

Really? Jacob had cancer? She finished drying her hands.

She couldn't help it. Her legs took her straight to the door of the treatment room.

'Jacob has cancer?' Her voice cracked. She could barely get the words out; her eyes were already filling with tears.

Hope and Isabel's heads shot around—a look of horror on both of their faces. They exchanged shocked glances.

Isabel took a step forward. 'Bonnie, I'm sorry. We didn't see you there.' She looked panicked. 'We should never have said anything.'

Her head was spinning. This almost felt as if it were happening to someone else.

Under any other circumstances she might think they were gossiping. But these women were Jacob's friends. They'd known him longer than she had and it was likely he'd taken them into his confidence.

'But you said it because you care—because Jacob is your friend.' Her heart was thudding against her chest.

Hope stepped forward too. She shook her head. 'Please

understand, this happened long before you got here. We were both sworn to secrecy. No one else knows. Jacob didn't want anyone to know he had non-Hodgkin's lymphoma, or that he was undergoing treatment.'

Bonnie felt her blood run cold. Non-Hodgkin's lymphoma. The same type of cancer that his mother had died from. Oh, no. Poor Jacob.

She could be sick, right now, all over the treatment-room floor.

Hope touched her arm. 'Are you okay? You look terrible, Bonnie. I'm so sorry. I knew something was going on between you and Jacob. I just didn't know what. I guess I thought he might tell you.'

She started to shake, but whether it was from shock or disbelief she just didn't know. She took a long, slow breath.

Pieces in her brain started to slot into place. Now she knew why he'd been evasive. Now she knew exactly why he'd been acting the way he had. Everything made sense to her.

But he hadn't told her. And that hurt. It hurt so much she wanted to grab him and shake him.

Isabel stepped over next to them both. 'Bonnie,' she said carefully, 'I can see you're upset. I have no idea what's going on with you two—but I want you to know. You're good for Jacob. Up until a few days ago he was the happiest I've ever seen him. If you can help him, then please do.' She glanced at Hope. 'He's our friend. Above everything, we want him to be happy and well. Things that we've got no control over.'

She squeezed Bonnie's arm. 'I think you may be an influencing factor over one of those things.'

The tears welled in Bonnie's eyes. 'But he didn't tell

me. He told me some things, but he never mentioned this at all.'

A worried glance shot between Hope and Isabel and Bonnie took another deep breath, trying to calm her frantic brain. 'But I think I know why.'

She turned on her heel and walked out of the door. The labour suite might be busy, but she wasn't looking after a patient right now and there were more than enough staff on shift.

Jacob had to be her priority.

Her footsteps halted a little on the way down the corridor. She'd spent the last two days fretting over herself. Thinking only about herself and Freya. She hadn't actually stopped to think that something might be wrong with Jacob. She'd challenged him. She'd asked him to tell her what was wrong. But not in a loving, compassionate way. She'd asked him in an angry, recriminatory kind of way. No wonder he hadn't told her.

She'd been too busy worrying about making a mistake again—focusing on the past instead of the future. How wrong she'd been. News like this put everything into perspective and made her realise exactly how precious life was.

She stalked past the midwives' station and opened the door of his office. He hadn't been around all day, but he was here now, sitting behind his desk.

Was he paler than normal? Were those dark circles under his eyes?

He jumped to his feet as soon as he saw her.

Now she could see him standing in front of her she could feel the adrenaline course through her. He could have told her. He could have told her the truth, couldn't he? Why hadn't he told her?

She'd been thinking a whole host of other things—

she'd thought the worst of him. When she'd had no right to. Jacob had been nothing but kind and supportive to her and Freya. And she'd pushed him away with her own insecurities. But instead of reaching out to her, he'd pushed her away too. What were the reasons for that?

This man had wound his way around her heart. She'd seen another side to him, a warm and loving side. A side that showed her, even if he didn't know it, he was ready to move on with his life.

He'd lit something inside her that she hadn't felt in years.

'Bonnie? Is there an emergency? Is something wrong with a patient?'

He was ready to run to the attention of any patient that needed him. But what about her?

She closed the door quietly behind her and folded her arms across her chest. She would not cry. *She would not cry.*

But her heart was squeezing in her chest. Jacob had cancer. Jacob had the same cancer that he'd watched his mother die from. She already knew the damage that had inflicted on him as a child, and in turn as an adult. But she'd only known half the story.

What had the test results shown?

'Nothing's wrong with a patient, Jacob.'

Confusion flooded his face. 'Then, what is it?'

'Something's wrong with me.' She pointed her finger. 'Something's wrong with you.' Frustration was building in her chest. 'Why didn't you tell me you had non-Hodgkin's? Why didn't you tell me you had the same type of cancer as your mother?'

This not-crying thing wasn't going to work. The tears were threatening to fall any second.

His mouth opened but no words came out. He sagged

down into his chair as if she'd just knocked the wind from his sails. 'Who told you?'

She pulled out the chair opposite and sat down. 'It doesn't matter who told me, Jacob. What matters is why *you* didn't?'

He still couldn't speak. He just shook his head for a few seconds, then put up his hands. 'How could I tell you, Bonnie? We've just met. I never expected this. I never expected to meet someone who would just—'

'Just what?'

His eyes met hers. There were no barriers in place. No shields to hide behind. 'Who would make me want to love again—to be part of a family again.'

She couldn't speak. A wave of emotion welled up inside her. This time a tear did escape, sliding down her cheek.

'I'm so sorry. I'm sorry I didn't stop to think what was wrong.' She shook her head. 'I just thought I was making a mistake again, that I didn't really know you that well.' She lifted her head and looked into his eyes. 'I felt as if I couldn't trust my judgement,' was all she could say. 'When all the time I knew what kind of man you were. I just didn't realise. I didn't think you might actually be sick.'

He stood up, walking around the desk and crouching down in front of her. He reached up and touched her hand, enveloping it with his. 'I had to wait, Bonnie. I had to know for sure. I couldn't put you and Freya through what I experienced as a kid. We'd only just met. I couldn't possibly expect you to sign up for that.'

She reached over and touched his cheeks. 'But you can, Jacob. I'm here for you. We're here for you. I don't care that you're sick. All I care about is that we're together.'

He reached up and brushed the tear from her cheek, taking one of her hands again. 'But why would I put someone that I love through that?' His face was serious. 'Two people that I love?'

The heat from his hand was rushing around her body. A whole host of tingles shooting straight towards her heart. 'You do?'

She couldn't help but smile. She hadn't been wrong. She hadn't imagined the connection between them. On one hand it was pure relief, on the other, she still couldn't understand why he wouldn't share with her.

'I do,' he said sincerely. 'I really do.'

She was fixed on his intense green eyes. 'Then why didn't you tell me, Jacob? You told me about your mum—why didn't you tell me about you?'

He ran one hand through his hair, giving his head a shake again. 'How could I tell you that, Bonnie? How can I declare love one minute, then tell you I've got a potential death sentence the next? What kind of man would do that to you? What kind of a man would do that to Freya?'

She held her breath. She understood. She understood exactly what he was saying but it still wasn't what she wanted to hear.

'So why couldn't we have that discussion, Jacob? I thought you didn't care about us at all. Why do you think I arranged to move out? Did you really think I wanted to?' She reached over and touched his jawline, feeling his smooth skin under her fingertips. 'Did you really think I would want to walk away if things were going to be tough? Because I wouldn't, Jacob. Not in a heartbeat. I love you. I don't care if it gets tough. I want to be the person by your side, holding your hand.'

His voice was quiet. 'But I don't want that for Freya. I don't want that for you. I watched my mother waste away before my eyes, the life just drained out of her. In the end, it wasn't a life at all. I could never do that to Freya. You've been through enough already.' He paused for a second then met her gaze again as he pulled his hand away from hers. 'I still can't.'

Bonnie leaned forwards; her face was inches from his. He could see fire spark behind her bright blue eyes. 'You don't get to make that choice any more, Jacob.' She pushed her hand up to her heart. '*I* do.'

He opened his mouth to speak again but she held up her hand. 'You've told me that you love me. You told me that you love Freya too. That's enough, Jacob. That's enough for me. I left because I doubted myself. I doubted my judgement. My past experience has made me untrusting, and I'm sorry for that.'

He pulled back. 'I can't do this. I can't let you do this. My mother had this cancer. I've had this cancer. I've got to assume that it's somehow in my genes. I can't make you any guarantees. I can't offer you what you want, Bonnie. Not when there's such a high risk.'

She stood up from the chair and faced him. 'What is it that I want?'

He frowned. 'Children. You'll want more children. This has to be in my genes. I could never, ever live with myself if I passed this disease on to our children.'

Bonnie looked furious. 'Have you asked me that? Have we had that conversation? What about what I think?'

He shook his head again. 'Look at you, Bonnie. You thrive on being a mother. You *love* being a mother—and you're fantastic at it. You were born to be a mother. I know that you want a whole house full of children. Don't pretend otherwise.' He pointed to his chest. 'And I can't give you that. I just can't.'

She blinked and he could see more unshed tears behind her eyes. 'I want you, Jacob. You and Freya. That's what I want. That's who I want my family to be. Can't we just work on that? Can't we just work on making a life together with what we have between us?' She stepped forwards, reaching up and cupping his cheek in her hand. 'Tell me about your test results. Tell me what happened. Good news or bad, I'm here for you. We're here for you. Just trust me enough to tell me.'

It was the first thing he'd noticed about her. Those bright blue eyes. And they were fixed on him with such an intensity right now that it felt as if a fist had closed around his heart and squeezed tight. He'd never felt like this. He'd never loved someone as he loved Bonnie. He'd never wanted to put himself on the line before. But Bonnie was everything. She didn't know. She didn't know he'd had good results. She didn't care. She still wanted to be with him.

For the first time he stopped to think straight. To let his heart rule his head. Every rational part of his brain had told him to back away. Every part of him that loved her didn't want her to be hurt.

But, for the first time, he could see himself building a life with Bonnie and Freya. A life that wasn't overshadowed with the thought of cancer recurring. A life that might actually be filled with love and hope.

And from the determined look in Bonnie's eyes it was exactly what she wanted.

His hand covered hers. 'My results were good, Bonnie. The non-Hodgkin's is in remission—for now. I'll need to keep having checks every six months for the next five years. There's always a chance it could recur.' As he said the words out loud he felt relief flood through him. He hadn't let that happen yet. He hadn't stopped to take a breath. The big black cloud that had been hanging over him for the last fourteen months had finally gone.

She didn't hesitate. She flung her arms around his neck. 'Oh, Jacob. That's fantastic.'

Her body was pressed against his. The warm angles familiar. The feeling of warmth, the feeling of love, the feeling of compassion were all here. All his for the taking. Could he really walk away from Bonnie now? When she'd told him no matter what his results she wanted to be by his side?

He stopped and pulled back, running his hand through her auburn hair. 'It is, isn't it?'

He was feeling lighter. And it wasn't just the diagnosis. It was the feeling of sharing. The feeling of having someone else invested in him. Of not having to face the future alone.

Bonnie's grin reached from ear to ear. 'It's better than fantastic.' She jumped up on him, her hands already around his neck, her legs now around his waist. The force sent him backwards against the wall and he started to laugh. Really laugh. Laugh as he hadn't in the last few years.

'Get rid of me now, Dr Layton,' she joked, her eyes gleaming.

This. This was what he wanted. This was what he'd wanted from the moment he'd seen her. Was he brave enough to reach out and grab it—just the way Bonnie had?

He was still smiling but he put on his most serious voice. 'Sister Reid, you seem to have put me in a compromising position.'

She tilted her head to one side. 'I have, haven't I? So, what are you going to do about it?' There was a challenge in her voice. 'I've already told you. Your choices are limited.' She uncoiled one hand from his neck and stroked her finger down his cheek. 'I think it's my job, and Freya's, to make sure that this year you have the happiest Christmas ever—*we* have the happiest Christmas ever.' The seriousness left her voice. 'So, what are you going to do, then?'

'Oh, that's easy,' he said as he adjusted her in his arms. 'I'm going to kiss you.'

And he did. Over and over again.

EPILOGUE

One year later

'ARE YOU READY, MUMMY?' Freya was bouncing up and down in her calf-length emerald-green bridesmaid dress.

Bonnie picked up her Christmas-themed bouquet and smiled. 'Oh, I've never been more ready. Let's go, gorgeous.'

They held hands and walked out of the hotel room to the top of the stairs. Jacob was standing at the bottom, waiting for them. In her honour, he'd dressed in a kilt. And she'd never seen a more handsome honorary Scotsman.

Her steps had never been surer as she picked up the skirts of her wedding dress and walked down the stairs to meet the man who made her complete.

Her last wedding hadn't felt anything like this. It had been beautiful, but she hadn't felt love in her heart and soul the way she did today. Jacob hadn't taken his eyes off her on her whole way down the stairs.

Her friends from the hospital applauded as she reached the bottom and she let out a nervous laugh. Jacob leaned over to kiss her. 'You look gorgeous,' he whispered.

'I don't think you're supposed to do that until after the ceremony,' she murmured back.

He smiled. 'Well, don't tell anyone. But I've got a really take-charge wife-to-be. She's taught me just to seize the moment.'

And she had. They'd spent the last year growing together as a family. Taking steps that she'd never have even considered a few years ago.

The celebrant gave them a nod towards the room where the wedding was to take place. The whole hotel was decorated for Christmas. A large Christmas tree was next to them at the bottom of the stairs and dark green and red garlands decorated the stairs. Twinkling lights glistened all around them. It really was the perfect setting.

'I'm not finished yet.' Jacob smiled.

'What do you mean?' she asked. This wasn't in the plans. But her tiny wave of panic disappeared in an instant. Whatever it was that Jacob wanted to do—she was sure she would love it.

'Before we start,' he said to their surrounding guests, 'I'd like to let you into a little secret.' He glanced at her. 'Bonnie and I have been keeping secrets from you—but even my future wife doesn't know this one.'

Her stomach flip-flopped. What was he talking about?

He pulled an envelope from inside his highland dress jacket. 'This morning, we received the news that we've been waiting for.' He gave her a smile that made her toes tingle. 'I haven't even had a chance to tell Bonnie yet, because I've been keeping with the wedding tradition of not seeing the bride before the ceremony.'

He held up the envelope. 'We got news this morning that Bonnie and I have been approved as adoptive parents.' He bent down and picked up Freya. 'Do you know that little brother or sister we've been talking about?'

She nodded solemnly. 'Well, some time next year you'll get to be a big sister.'

'I will?'

'We will?' Bonnie could hardly contain her excitement. They'd been waiting for the final verdict. And this just made the whole day even more perfect.

A number of waiters appeared with trays of champagne that were quickly dispersed amongst the guests. Jacob handed one to Bonnie. He held his aloft. 'So, we've not even made it to the altar yet. But I guess I decided to seize the moment.' She could see the glint in his eyes as he spoke.

'Can I ask you all to raise your glasses? To the best Christmas ever and to families.'

Bonnie clinked her glass with his and took a sip, then wrapped her arms around him and Freya. 'You're going to make me cry.' She laughed. 'And we're not even married yet.' She gave her head a little shake. 'This couldn't be more perfect.'

His green eyes fixed on hers. 'Oh, yes, it could,' he said as he bent to kiss her. 'Happy Christmas, Mrs Layton.'

* * * * *

MILLS & BOON®
Hardback – November 2015

ROMANCE

A Christmas Vow of Seduction	Maisey Yates
Brazilian's Nine Months' Notice	Susan Stephens
The Sheikh's Christmas Conquest	Sharon Kendrick
Shackled to the Sheikh	Trish Morey
Unwrapping the Castelli Secret	Caitlin Crews
A Marriage Fit for a Sinner	Maya Blake
Larenzo's Christmas Baby	Kate Hewitt
Bought for Her Innocence	Tara Pammi
His Lost-and-Found Bride	Scarlet Wilson
Housekeeper Under the Mistletoe	Cara Colter
Gift-Wrapped in Her Wedding Dress	Kandy Shepherd
The Prince's Christmas Vow	Jennifer Faye
A Touch of Christmas Magic	Scarlet Wilson
Her Christmas Baby Bump	Robin Gianna
Winter Wedding in Vegas	Janice Lynn
One Night Before Christmas	Susan Carlisle
A December to Remember	Sue MacKay
A Father This Christmas?	Louisa Heaton
A Christmas Baby Surprise	Catherine Mann
Courting the Cowboy Boss	Janice Maynard

MILLS & BOON®
Large Print – November 2015

ROMANCE

The Ruthless Greek's Return	Sharon Kendrick
Bound by the Billionaire's Baby	Cathy Williams
Married for Amari's Heir	Maisey Yates
A Taste of Sin	Maggie Cox
Sicilian's Shock Proposal	Carol Marinelli
Vows Made in Secret	Louise Fuller
The Sheikh's Wedding Contract	Andie Brock
A Bride for the Italian Boss	Susan Meier
The Millionaire's True Worth	Rebecca Winters
The Earl's Convenient Wife	Marion Lennox
Vettori's Damsel in Distress	Liz Fielding

HISTORICAL

A Rose for Major Flint	Louise Allen
The Duke's Daring Debutante	Ann Lethbridge
Lord Laughraine's Summer Promise	Elizabeth Beacon
Warrior of Ice	Michelle Willingham
A Wager for the Widow	Elisabeth Hobbes

MEDICAL

Always the Midwife	Alison Roberts
Midwife's Baby Bump	Susanne Hampton
A Kiss to Melt Her Heart	Emily Forbes
Tempted by Her Italian Surgeon	Louisa George
Daring to Date Her Ex	Annie Claydon
The One Man to Heal Her	Meredith Webber

MILLS & BOON®
Hardback – December 2015

ROMANCE

MILLS & BOON®
Large Print – December 2015

ROMANCE

The Greek Demands His Heir	Lynne Graham
The Sinner's Marriage Redemption	Annie West
His Sicilian Cinderella	Carol Marinelli
Captivated by the Greek	Julia James
The Perfect Cazorla Wife	Michelle Smart
Claimed for His Duty	Tara Pammi
The Marakaios Baby	Kate Hewitt
Return of the Italian Tycoon	Jennifer Faye
His Unforgettable Fiancée	Teresa Carpenter
Hired by the Brooding Billionaire	Kandy Shepherd
A Will, a Wish...a Proposal	Jessica Gilmore

HISTORICAL

Griffin Stone: Duke of Decadence	Carole Mortimer
Rake Most Likely to Thrill	Bronwyn Scott
Under a Desert Moon	Laura Martin
The Bootlegger's Daughter	Lauri Robinson
The Captain's Frozen Dream	Georgie Lee

MEDICAL

Midwife...to Mum!	Sue MacKay
His Best Friend's Baby	Susan Carlisle
Italian Surgeon to the Stars	Melanie Milburne
Her Greek Doctor's Proposal	Robin Gianna
New York Doc to Blushing Bride	Janice Lynn
Still Married to Her Ex!	Lucy Clark

MILLS & BOON®

Why shop at millsandboon.co.uk?

Each year, thousands of romance readers find their perfect read at millsandboon.co.uk. That's because we're passionate about bringing you the very best romantic fiction. Here are some of the advantages of shopping at www.millsandboon.co.uk:

* **Get new books first**—you'll be able to buy your favourite books one month before they hit the shops

* **Get exclusive discounts**—you'll also be able to buy our specially created monthly collections, with up to 50% off the RRP

* **Find your favourite authors**—latest news, interviews and new releases for all your favourite authors and series on our website, plus ideas for what to try next

* **Join in**—once you've bought your favourite books, don't forget to register with us to rate, review and join in the discussions

Visit **www.millsandboon.co.uk**
for all this and more today!

MILLS_WEB_HB